ANCIENT TERROR

Worse than darkness were the words that kept running over and over through Broco's head, sending fingers of icy dread through his drumming heart.

His Father's words came back to him now, vividly, as if he were sitting before the talking fire dogs in front of his own home hearth, listening with eager attention as the history of Dwarfdom was recited.

"And when it came to pass that the Enemy had entered into being, the Dwarfdom of olden began to retreat. The Enemy was crafty and treacherous, and began to plant the seeds of doubt and mistrust through all Creation. And as later Lords Underearth came into power, the Guardians were called up, to protect the entries and highways into the kingdoms underground."

Broco shuddered, and clasped the Chest closer to his pounding heart . . . and wondered how he might ever pass those all-powerful and pitiless Guardians . . . how he might ever escape the Enemy who now had him in the jaws of a closing trap . . .

The Circle of Light Series

by Niel Hancock

Available from
WARNER BOOKS

Circle of Light ~3
Calix Stay
by Niel Hancock

WARNER BOOKS

A Warner Communications Company

For Kathlene Collins
who knew of whales and Ahabs.

WARNER BOOKS EDITION

Copyright © 1977 by Niel Hancock.
All rights reserved.

Warner Books, Inc.,
666 Fifth Avenue,
New York, N.Y. 10103

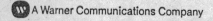 A Warner Communications Company

Printed in the United States of America

First Warner Books Printing: December, 1982

10 9 8 7 6 5 4 3 2 1

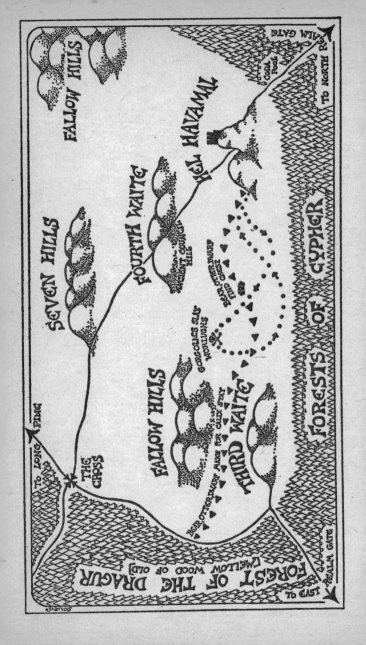

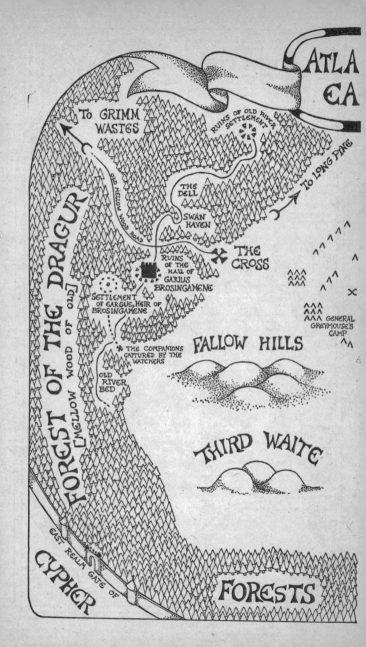

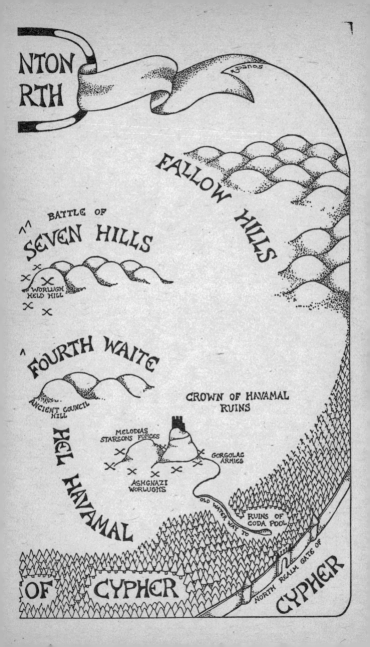

THE ROAD TO GRIMM

PURSUIT

⊠ As the companions raced on, a bomb burst behind them, and flung stinging hot particles of sand and iron shards all about them. Bear moaned in pain, but kept his pace, and Flewingam began to limp from the burning fire in his left leg.

Dwarf ran headfirst into a tall, gaunt man, dressed in a gray-green tunic and trousers, and carrying a great crossbow made of ebony wood. Cranfallow tried to raise his firearm, but a powerful hand wrenched it from his grasp, a bright light flashed in his head, and he sank into an unknowing darkness.

Dwarf was knocked breathless by his sudden collision with the grim warrior, and sat stunned at his feet.

The forest behind them had gone ominously silent.

Flewingam and Thinvoice came crashing up,

unable to see until too late the gray figure, the fallen form of Cranfallow, and Dwarf sitting helpless before him on the ground. Bear skidded into the clearing, blowing hard.

The tall warrior did not speak, but stared coldly at the friends. They were transfixed by the harsh blue eyes that glowered at them from beneath dark brows, in a face that seemed ravished by wind and weather, turned to the almost black color of the deadly-looking weapon he held.

Without a sound, a grim ring of men who looked like the first appeared around the dumbfounded comrades.

Before the stunned companions could move to defend themselves, tiny black darts whirred from the bows of the ring of silent soldiers, and bright spinning darkness settled over their eyes and odd music began to play.

In a moment it was over.

And Otter, who had fallen into the depths of an old trap, unused and overgrown with sharp thorn brakes, lay motionless and undetected.

CAPTURED

Dwarf's arms ached from the bonds that bit
cruelly into his wrists. His head thumped with
the rough jostling, and a heavy darkness veiled
his eyes whenever he dared open them. It took
him a few seconds to realize he was being carried roughly along, slung under a steely arm
that gripped him until his breath came in shallow gulps. Gazing wildly about, he saw they
were still in the shadows of the forest, only now
the trees drew close together, and seemed to
form a solid wall of black, ominous wood.

Bear stumbled and fell beside him for a moment, then was prodded to his feet by a silent
guard. The big animal's paws were held together by a leather thong, and an iron collar
circled his neck, attached to a length of chain
held by a swift-striding man in front of him.
Bear's eyes rolled listlessly, and his huge head
swung dully from side to side as he walked.

Broco's reeling mind tried to turn back the events, to remember what had happened, but his head throbbed with leaden pain, and he lost consciousness, struggling vainly to free himself from his captors.

The man who held Bear's chain laughed suddenly and jerked viciously on the iron leash. Bear fell forward and began walking on all fours.

"There's more to these brutes than meets the eye, Gymir. Who would have thought this one could take the form of a dancing bear?"

"It will please Garius. He has had no magicians to amuse him in years. He's as fond of a conjurer as his father was."

"Anything that pleases him takes his mind off keeping us out on these endless patrols. There's nothing left to guard but soot and ashes, anyhow."

The first man, lighter and younger than his companion, jerked roughly on the leash that held Bear.

"As for me, I'd let those halfmen have it," said Gymir. "No one but the likes of them would want it."

"But it's better than outside. They have worse generals than Garius."

"It isn't the same, though. I've never seen farther than a bowshot beyond these woods."

"They were beautiful in their time. I've heard the old ones speak of the years before the wars."

"Bah," spat Bear's captor, "fireside tales."

"Perhaps so, but you'd best mind how you

speak around Garius, or the others. Your loose talk would have you banished." Gymir paused to let the thought sink in. "And you know what that means."

"Death is nothing to the boredom here. I'd almost welcome it, as a change."

Gymir laughed, and thrust the limp body of Dwarf into an easier load.

"If it's entertainment you want, we have all the makings of a good show here with us."

Hoder studied the chained Bear and the lifeless figure of Dwarf, and the three men who marched in shackles before them.

"I wouldn't call it much," he said grudgingly, "but at least it will keep us off these endless, wasted patrols for a day or two."

"Or longer, if any of the others have tricks as good as your friend there."

"I've seen better," yawned Hoder. "The witch that lives in the Ruins is more diverting."

"You mean her brew is more appealing," teased Gymir.

"It keeps your mind off dull duty and the pointless jokes of Garius."

"Shhhhh," cautioned Gymir, "the sergeant is coming."

The gaunt figure that Dwarf had collided with dropped back along the line of prisoners until he was abreast of Bear.

"So our magician finds our elixir potent enough to take the sting from his temper, does he?"

"I doubt if he feels the march as much as I," said Hoder, pulling the leash taunt.

The sergeant pulled Dwarf's head up brusquely, and looked briefly at the lolling, unconscious face.

"I've not seen the likes of him since I was but a cadet. We found a troop of them camped below Ravens Fen."

"Were they more lively than this lout?" asked Hoder.

"So lively we ended up slaying a dozen of them. Even our stunning darts didn't seem to faze them. This fellow seems to be of a less vigorous heritage than those devils."

"What sport did you find in them?" questioned Gymir, hoping his burden would prove worthy of his efforts.

"They rebuilt the lower hall. That's what you see now of the Ruins. And they had a fancy way with metals. Most of our arrow tips and knives are their craft."

"It would be simpler to arm ourselves like our friends here," complained Hoder, hefting the firearm he had taken from Bear.

"You know what Garius thinks of those things, Private Hoder. And they can't stun, only kill." The sergeant glared at the man with his icy blue eyes before going on. "They wouldn't serve our purpose as well, and they aren't as silent as our crossbows."

"What does it matter now who knows we're in these woods? It's no secret to them outside."

Hoder held the sergeant's frigid glance, then looked away.

"We'll see about this when we're home, Pri-

vate. I think we shall have a long talk about
your odd ideas."

The older man quickened his pace, and without further word, he moved to the head of the
column.

"Now you've cut it, you blind ass. You've
smart-talked your way into a breach-of-conduct
hearing."

"It won't come to that," replied Hoder. "I
happen to know a few things of our dauntless
leader."

"Like what?" asked Gymir, unbelieving.

"Like the fact he was born outside."

Gymir ground to a halt, and stared
speechless at his friend.

"No one knows except me and the witch. She
told me a long time ago. And she also told me
that Garius isn't really the blood son of Brosingamene. At least not in legal wedlock."

Gymir's eyes grew wide, and he stammered
something inaudible.

"You like to think of your leaders as above us
common lot, but they find their pleasures the
same as you or me." Hoder laughed a low, ugly
laugh. "Garius' daddy had a sweetheart on the
sly that lived in the old river settlement near
Swans Haven. As pretty as a spring flower, and
the daughter of one of his stonecutters. Garius
was born from her, and stayed in the river settlement until his daddy's wife died, then he
brought Garius and his pretty mama to live at
court."

"A pack of lies," growled Gymir. "A lie the

witch has told you and made you believe. It's
that evil wine she mixes."

"Is it? Maybe you should see for yourself."
Hoder smiled slyly from the corner of his face.

"I don't believe it," Gymir said firmly.

"Then come with me to see. The witch is
Garius' mother, and she can prove it."

"And how can she do that? She's been banished from court, so she would carry a grief
and want to hurt Garius if she could." Gymir's
face closed into a doubting scowl. "What proof
has she?"

"Aha," shot Hoder, triumphant. "Then you
doubt."

"Not doubt. I just wonder at it."

"And well you should, my friend. Why do
you think she lives in the Ruins, while we have
set up our settlement beyond the Dell? Why
shouldn't Garius have stayed, and sent her
away?"

"The Ruins aren't fit to live in," said Gymir
simply.

"But it could have been made livable with
far less work than building anew."

"I don't see what you're driving at, Hoder.
There is enough corruption at court without
you spreading ugly rumors about to stir up
more trouble."

"She lives there because Garius' father put it
in contract that she should dwell there as long
as she lived. And she shall outlive us all, at the
rate she's going now."

Hoder laughed again, and dragged Bear
roughly on.

"Dangerous talk, Hoder. You'll start something more than you'll bargain for."

"We'll see," said Hoder cryptically.

Otter, after escaping from his earthen prison, crept silently along in the thickets that bordered both sides of the faint trail the men followed. His limbs ached from the bruises he had suffered in his fall, but his mind flamed in bright anger as he looked at his friends, enslaved and held under some strange spell. They seemed hardly to know they were alive, and Otter could not believe Bear would let himself be treated in such a way if he were himself.

The little animal scurried along at a good pace in order to keep these strange foemen in sight. He must rescue his friends, he knew, but his mind went blank every time he tried to formulate a plan that would free them. And he wasn't sure what power held them, or even if they would know him if he tried to save them. He knew he couldn't hope to free them alone, and that he would need their help, but not one of his friends even seemed to be aware of breathing, or walking.

After what seemed like hours, the strange warriors disappeared into a wall of green, and Otter stared in disbelief.

They had simply vanished.

SOLDIERS
OF BROSINGAMENE

"Who goes?" rang out an invisible voice.

"Wood Patrol Two," answered the gaunt sergeant.

"Pass," came the voice of the unseen sentry.

Otter heard the voices, and knew they weren't far away. He tested his nose and followed the man scent up to the solid wall of green, and found to his surprise that it was fashioned by man, and cleverly disguised to look like natural growth. It seemed to be vines and ropes woven into a mesh of leaves and branches, but it was solid all along its side, and there was no way to slip through, so thickly woven was it. Otter was sure the sentry he had heard had some way of detecting someone slipping through, so he searched on in hopes of finding a way over or under this wall that cut him off from his captured companions.

He started slowly down the green fence, then

checked himself suddenly. There not a paw's distance away was another pit, concealed to look like a part of the forest floor.

"They're overly fond of digging, for Mankind," mused Otter, half aloud.

He cautiously stepped around the trap, then stopped again.

He thrust his nose under the leaf cover, rooting about until he could make out the dark depths below. It was as he had dared let himself hope. The pit spanned both sides of the fence, one half on the outside, and the other portion beyond the barrier.

"I'd give a whisker or two if this were a river," he lamented to himself. "But then I must find some way to help my friends."

And thinking of the cruel bonds that held Bear and Dwarf, and Flewingam, Ned, and Cranfallow, Otter wrinkled up his nose and plunged doggedly on, clawing for paw holds, hearing the dirt he loosened falling, and then the noise as it hit bottom, far below. He frightened himself badly twice, almost letting go his grip as he slowly inched toward the far side of the pit, but at last, winded and puffing, he drew himself carefully up, peered around quickly, and emerged within the barricades of the strange enemy.

He went softly along the inside of the woven fence, looking for some sign of the sentry he had heard, but nothing seemed to move in the dense wood, now grown darker, as if coming into this walled place shut out everything, even the sun.

He crept on, until at length he thought he could make out what looked to be an ancient tree, its broad trunk many feet across, and after studying it for a while, he could see there were slits cut at intervals, and a darker shadow showed the outline of a small door.

A cough from inside the tree itself convinced Otter he had discovered the hidden watcher.

He skirted around the sentry, and when he felt it was safe, he returned to the faint track that led on deeper into the very heart of the dense wood, which now, on this side of the strange border, seemed to grow green again, and the black color of the trunks turned a warmer color, and there were small lawns of grass here and there, and for the first time since he had entered this hateful place, Otter saw what looked to be small, dark red flowers.

"I wonder what manner of men these are," murmured Otter, whistling softly to himself. "They seem to look of the right sort, but why would they shoot the Worlughs and put Bear and Dwarf and the others under some sort of spell and tie them up?"

As he went on, he heard the faint hum of voices from a distance, and slowed his pace, and sought deeper shadows beyond the trail to shield him from any prying eyes.

The voices grew clearer, all in a tongue he understood well, and he grew more puzzled at the strange men's behavior. They spoke in the manner of High Mankind—men of the races who were upon Atlanton Earth from the Golden Ages—with no trace of lisp or slur, and

Otter was sure he had seen men of this sort at
times, in the war camps of Greymouse and
Melodias.

A great commotion jerked his attention
toward the voices, near enough now to hear
them clearly.

"What a prize, eh, Jokim? A performing bear,
and one of the runt kind. And three strong
backs to help us with our canals."

"Aye, a prize indeed. Garius will find reason
to hold a high feast tonight. Then we can see
the bear dance, or juggle, or whatever he does.
Is the runt of a minstrel kind?"

"I don't know," replied the man called Jokim.
"We caught them in the wood, down below the
Old River. We slew ten of the beast tribe, too.
They seemed to be after our fine fellows here."

"Hoder says the bear is a magician. Is there
any truth to his words?"

"For once, yes. He changed from man to
bear right before us, and reared and swarmed
Alud and Diel with claws and fangs gleaming
like fire, but we got a stun dart into him quick
enough. Even a big one like that is no match
for that herb."

"Did you get all of them, or did some of their
party escape?"

Otter's heart stopped, and he crouched lower
in his hiding place.

"We caught all we saw. I sent a scouting
party to scour the area, but there was nothing
more but the dead beasts."

Otter slid along on his stomach until he
reached a low building, brown and with a

green thatched roof, that stood close by the edge of the forest. He crept on, past another structure, and peered gingerly over the boards of a small fence that ran around the border of a flower garden, full of the small red flowers he had seen on his way in.

He saw that all the houses were of the same shape, all the pleasant brown earth color, built low to the ground, with the green thatched eaves of the roofs low enough that he could have stood and touched them. From where he lay, it seemed there were many of these buildings, and they ran in a great form of a circle that he could not see the end of. In the center of this circle were the people, and they ringed what looked to be a tall stone pillar, set upon a broad slab of tree stump. It was even larger than the tree that hid the sentry, and if the tree had been as high as its width indicated, it must have towered far beyond all the other trees of the wood in its day.

A vague thought kept racing through Otter's mind, but he could not keep it still long enough to focus on it, and his anger at seeing his friends in their bonds flared within him, and he gnashed his teeth in fury at his helplessness.

"But there must be a way," he chittered angrily. "They would find themselves in a fine pickle if Froghorn or Greyfax were here."

His hopes rose at the thought of the wizards, but quickly vanished. They would have no way of knowing of the companions' danger, and he had no way to call them.

His breathing stopped, and his eyes grew wide.

The Chest.

The Chest was in danger, although he did not think these warriors had been interested in anything but the idea of finding some entertaining diversions to amuse themselves with. They didn't seem the proper types to be of the Dark Queen's armies, nor yet did they appear to be of the Light. In truth, they spoke nothing at all to hint at their leader, other than the name Garius, or a name similar to that.

The vague thought flickered through his mind again.

He repeated the name he had heard over and over, but nothing came.

A horn blew a high, trilling call, and a new group of people came into view.

These men had blood-red tunics with silver vests, with tall black boots that were like mirrors. The men wore dark blue trousers, and their feet moved in time to a small drum that beat in the back of the procession.

As Otter watched, the red tunics passed, then came pale-faced ladies, fair, but not anything near as fair as Cybelle or Lorini. They wore light blue dresses, and had servants that carried the trains of their long gowns.

After the women came a tall man, gray-haired and dressed in dark blue from his neck to his boots. He had a drooping gray mustache that hung past his chin, and fiery blue eyes that crackled like flaming ice.

As he passed, the crowd bowed low and uttered the name he had been saying in his head.

The man looked neither right nor left, but strode on, straight toward where his friends were tied.

Otter looked back at the pillar. Bear had slumped to the ground in a heavy stupor, and Dwarf was sitting beside him, head lolling as if in time to the drum. Flewingam, Cranfallow, and Ned Thinvoice were tied back to back a little distance away. Their eyes stared blankly at the mass of people that pushed close around them, gazing at them curiously.

Garius, for that is who this was, walked directly up to the man in charge of the prisoners.

"Well done, Jokim."

Jokim bowed low, and stepped aside so that his leader could inspect his catch.

"Is this the magician?" asked the man in blue, addressing no one in particular. He reached a hand out to touch Bear.

"I wouldn't do that, your honor. He came near killing two of us before we could subdue him."

"Harmless-looking now, wouldn't you say? Is he the magician?"

"Yes, your honor."

"Good. Take him along."

He motioned a finger, and Bear was dragged unresisting away.

"And this? What a specimen. There have been none of these halfmen seen hereabouts for ages. A delightful present to Her Excellency. He can amuse her with whatever it is he does."

"As you wish, your honor."

The cold bue eyes fell on Flewingam and his two companions.

"You may let them work the canals. I don't suppose they are anything but servant class?"

"They were with the magician and the half-man. We thought perhaps they served them, your honor."

"So. It looks as if there is cause for festivity this evening. Grand Marshal, announce there will be open court tonight. Dancing and wine."

Garius beckoned the sergeant to him.

"Jokim, you shall be guest major. You have served exceeding well. My congratulations."

"Thank you, your honor. I hope I have pleased you, sir."

"You have indeed, my loyal Jokim. I have been long without a cause to laugh until now."

He nodded, and as if on signal, the drum struck up, the red tunics swayed in time and began to move, followed by the retinue of the ladies, then Garius, and the procession swung once around the pillar, and back in the direction it had come.

Otter, after watching Bear be led away, had grown uneasy, and moved around more of the buildings, until he was on the side the procession passed when it returned. He stole quietly along at the circle's edge, close to the safety of the trees, and after a time, he saw his destination.

It was a great house, of the same style as all

the others, but its outward proportions were
gigantic. It appeared to Otter it was as large as
all the rest of the buildings put together, and a
tall doorway, with double gates, opened at its
front. He could see no windows, and the single
door seemed the only way to enter the dwelling.

The procession passed inside, and the great
gates swung shut, and Otter's heart sank. There
seemed to be no way for him to reach his
friends, no help he could give them if he did
manage to get inside.

A dark cloud of despair settled over him, and
the finality of it caused him to sit heavily down.

And there was an end of it. All prisoners,
even he, in the hands of a strange enemy, in
the very secret depths of the Dragur Wood.

He toyed with the idea of giving himself up,
for that way he would at least be with his
friends. He almost stood to reveal himself, but
that same nagging thought had crept back,
hammering at his senses until he forgot about
delivering himself to his enemies, and a tiny
spark of hope lightened the darkness that had
stolen over his heart.

The pillar of stone he had seen in the Coda
Pool.

Was this how it was to end, then? Was that
what the sacred well had told him? Lost forever in these black woods, as prisoners of a man
with cold blue eyes, who sought only amusement?

Then he remembered the pool had also
shown other things, and he was sure it meant

there were more things to come and they
would not end their long journey beneath
prison walls.

He would wait until dark, then make what
plans he could. But he knew he must hide and
remain free at all costs.

Somehow, he knew, he must save his friends.

GARIUS BROSINGAMENE
HOLDS A FEAST

A great crowd milled about the spacious central room in the Seat of Garius, Tenth Watcher of Amarigin, heir of the House of Brosingamene. Tall beams held the thatched roof, and intricate wood carving showed everywhere on rafter and support, of fierce dragon heads, and ogres, and gaunt, stone-faced men in mighty battle dress, with tall plumes on their savage-looking helmets.

The room was alive with golden candlelight, and reed lamps hissed softly over the noise of many voices talking and laughing. An air of excitement crackled through the gathering, and everyone's eyes kept returning to the curved archway that led into Lord Garius' inner court.

It was the first feast night to be held in many long, boring months.

Masks and gaily colored costumes fluttered and turned in the golden light, and lute music

spun a magic web of tension and excitement
over the nervous crowd.

At one darker corner of the room, a masked
figure stood apart, sipping from a carved
wooden cup and glancing anxiously at his surroundings.

Otter, in the mask of a boar, felt silly in the
ridiculous getup, but it had solved the difficult
task of gaining entrance to the dwelling that
imprisoned his friends.

Beside him, a lady tittered and flirted coyly
with her escort, then turned to speak.

"Marius?"

Sudden fear gripped Otter's heart.

"Cleon?" she chimed again, becoming interested in her game.

Otter shook his head, and murmured something barely audible.

"Justin," she cried, convinced he was indeed
the friend she named.

"Come on, let's find a place to dance."

Otter tried declining, but she began to look
angry, so he went reluctantly with her, until
they found the minstrels and edged their way
into the dancing square.

Fortunately the small space was very
crowded, and Otter was jostled about so that
no one could see that he did not know this
form of dance.

The lady kept speaking to him, but the noise
and bustle was too great for him to hear what
she said, and he kept trying to turn himself so
that he could watch the gate to the inner court.
He was sure it was from there Bear and Dwarf

would come. Of Ned Thinvoice and Cranfallow
and Flewingam he knew nothing. But he did
not think they were in the same prison.

Someone rudely bumped him, and Otter saw
a tall, angular man blocking him from the lady,
and addressing him in a rather loud, drunken
manner.

"So you've thought to entertain yourself with
Freya, eh?"

The slurred, wine-sodden voice was vaguely
familiar, but he had no time to place it, for the
man was shoving him back with an iron-hard
hand.

Otter easily sidestepped the man's attack,
and slipped into the mass of bodies around
him. As he shoved his way through the dancing
mob, he heard the loud, whining tone of the
woman over the music. She addressed him as
Gymir, and Otter remembered where he had
heard the voice. As he broke through the mill-
ing crowd, he heard the man's angry replies.

He was relieved to be once more free to
watch the archway, and to go unnoticed.

A fanfare of horns announced the master of
the house had arrived. Bows and curtsies and a
swell of voices accompanied the entrance of
Garius, dressed once more in solid blue, but of
a finer cut. As Otter bowed low to the strange
man, he saw the eyes were bright and cunning,
and the man seemed in a great state of agita-
tion.

After the proper respects were paid to the
lord of the house, a wild dance song burst forth
from the musicians, and a frenzied reel caught

everyone up into a whirling, spinning mass. Otter found himself drawn into a tight circle of red-faced dancers, their hands holding his in crushing grips, and he was flung crazily about in this oddly savage ritual.

Somewhere in his mind, he remembered the stately, rhythmic dances in the great hall of Cypher, and he was somehow saddened by that thought, and his heart ached to be once more near Cybelle, beyond these strange, hostile humans, with Bear, and Dwarf, and Ned, and Flewingam, and Cranfallow, safe from the dangers they were all now in.

As the music stopped, the revelers all broke into tumultous applause and laughter. When that had died down somewhat, Otter saw that Garius had ascended a raised platform at the far end of the room and now motioned for his followers to be silent.

Slowly the great hall quietened.

"My faithful subjects, tonight we have the pleasures of the feast before us."

This was met with approving applause.

"And due to the find work of Jokim, we shall have first-rate amusements this night."

More scattered applause and excited voices.

"So let us begin, with no further time devoted to talk."

The crowd clapped madly, and at once fell upon the low tables laden with food and wine.

Otter was pushed toward a seat by unseen hands, and he was trapped between two very old women, who turned their toothless smiles upon him and kept forcing pieces of food or cups of wine into his hands.

In his preoccupation, he did not notice Bear and Dwarf being led to the platform where Garius dined.

When he at last found time to look toward the archway, his eyes fell at once on his friends chained to a great block of stone before the master's table.

His spirits soared, for Bear glared about at his captors with a hatred so strong it made his guards uneasy, and they carefully kept out of reach of his deadly claws and fangs.

Dwarf stared sullenly straight ahead, ignoring the curious glances of the crowd that surrounded him.

Otter saw with relief that Broco still wore his dark green cloak, and reasoned that the Chest was yet safe.

A louder music filled the hall as a new group of musicians came into view, and many birds of bright colors were released from woven reed cages, to soar and fly about the upper regions of the rafters, flashing in mirrored rainbow hues as their wings caught the soft golden lights.

Otter's mind raced, searching for a plan that would free his friends, but the presence of so many enemy soldiers discouraged him, and the high hopes he had held slowly left him with a sinking heart.

Even if he could free Dwarf and Bear from their chains, these strange men had the spells they had used to capture them before, which had made even Bear's terrible wrath no more dangerous than the harmless birds that skated wildly about the smoky heights of the ceiling beams.

Before he had finished his bitter thought, an awed hush fell over the company, and he turned to see an ancient crone standing at the door, her clothes no more than tatters, her once proud face pitted and worn with extreme age.

A moan passed through the crowd, and many of the revelers began cautiously withdrawing from the feast tables.

Garius seemed paralyzed with fear and rage, and his face colored into a bluish mask.

The crone was the first to speak.

"Did you think you could exclude me, my fine master?"

"I did not, you leprous old hag."

"Ah, old hag, indeed. I've come to see your spell worker that you've caught."

"Then see, and be gone. You know you're breaking the code. You've been banished by the decree of the court. You could be slain for this breach."

"And who would dare raise a hand against me?"

The old woman wheezed into laughter, and scuttled forward.

People frantically cleared her path, until she stood at the platform, glaring up with watery eyes at Garius.

"You see? No one wants to harm me."

Garius turned bright crimson, and the veins in his throat stood out when he spoke.

"You are ordered from here, woman. I demand you take your leave."

"In time, my pretty, in time. I've come to see your toys, and see them I shall."

She hoisted herself with amazing agility onto the platform steps, and moved to confront Broco and Bear.

"I suppose these are your magicians?" she cackled, doubling over until her nose was almost on the floor.

Bear began a warning growl low in his throat, and Broco managed a halfhearted huff.

Otter squirmed his way closer to the platform.

"Let's see you perform, oh, master. Do you dance, or juggle, or sing?"

She doubled over again with her wheezing laugh.

"They shall perform, if you wish it," glowered Garius. "Then you shall depart my house."

The old woman gave a sly look in his direction.

"I would not press yet so hard, my pretty."

Her cackling seemed to push Garius near a fit.

"Guards," he hissed, his voice barely a whisper.

No one moved.

"I think I shall have these pretties, Garius," said the old woman. "They look to be much too dull for you. I don't think they are up to amusing your guests tonight."

Before Garius could move to stop her, she

had undone Bear and Dwarf, and beckoned them to follow her.

Otter watched in amazement as his two friends trailed tamely along behind her.

The Tenth Watcher of Amarigin made no move to stop the three as they wound their way through the hall.

Otter slipped quietly along behind, discarding his boar's head mask once he was clear of the hall and suspicious eyes, and he crept cautiously on beneath the dark stars as she moved through the low fence that bordered the settlement. Once beyond that, the woods grew wild and thick, and she led her oddly quiet captives still deeper into the growing gloom.

AN UNFORESEEN ALLY

⊠ Once, when he had accidentally allowed himself to get too close to the ancient crone, Otter heard her creaking voice speaking in a hushed whisper. He could not make out the words, but he thought, or imagined, that he heard Bear's mumbled reply, or Broco's huffed answer.

After they had gone what seemed miles in the dark wood, Otter came across the chains that had bound his friends.

Puzzled, yet easier, he followed on, out of sight or sound.

Otter saw what looked to be buildings against the deeper shadows around them rising from the black shadows ahead. As he neared, he saw it was indeed the rambling halls and towers of what appeared to be a great fortress.

A faintly glowing light shone weakly from

some window on the ground level, far inside
the walls and gates.

Otter lost sight of his friends, and had to
stop a moment to listen for the sound of footsteps.

"You may join us now, if you like, Master Otter," creaked the old voice. "It is easy to lose
one's way from now on."

Otter jumped, and cried out in shocked surprise as the ancient crone touched his arm.

"It's all right, old fellow," crooned Bear.
"We've heard you back there forever. You forget you don't go so quietly when you're in your
man form."

"Not that your galumphing about is any quieter when in your own shoes," grumped Dwarf,
remembering all the times Otter had sounded
like an army passing over a plain of rocks.

"You may as well come on and join us."

Dwarf suddenly stood at Otter's elbow.

"I will, thanks," chirped Otter, having
changed into his own form.

"But why didn't somebody let me know, before I barked my shins and ruffled my nose, that
I had nothing to hide from?"

"Because we were afraid of being followed
by worse than you," said Bear. "Alane wasn't
sure of your identity for a time."

"I am Alane," croaked the ancient woman,
"and I have awaited your coming for many
years."

Otter peered into the darkness, trying to
catch sight of the old woman's face.

"You mean you knew we were coming?" he blurted out, feeling more confused than ever.

"She knows Greyfax," explained Dwarf.

"Is he here?" asked Otter, brightening.

"No, not now. But he has been," the old woman said, "although it's been a long year since I've set eyes on his face."

Otter's hopes fell.

"She said Greyfax told her that there would be signs she was to watch for," went on Broco. "And that she was to wait for those who came in chains."

"But what are we going to do about Ned, Cranny, and Flewingam?" Otter asked, more and more puzzled. "We can't leave them here for slaves."

"They are in my hands," said Alane simply. "I had them sent to me earlier today."

"Won't Garius try to take us back? I mean, won't he be angry, and cause trouble?"

"I think not, Master Otter. Garius is a strong-willed man, but he dares not go against me. You see, I am his mother."

"Then what I heard is true?"

"To that effect, yes. Who spoke of this? Hoder?"

"I think that was his name."

"He is more to be feared than Garius, that one. He has come here often in the past, and discovered much that he might use to gain power over my son. I thought at first he was of a kindly nature, and pitied me, and tried to comfort me, but I know otherwise now."

"She thinks we should leave at first light,"

said Dwarf. "And if that is to be, we'd better find our plans and beds, and food."

"Of course. I've kept us long standing in the dark. I shall make you cots tonight, and gather food for your journey. And I've got a trick or two that might serve you as a plan."

Alane turned, and led the three companions over the broken wall of the old fortress, down many twisting ways, until at length they stood before a small window filled with light.

The solid wall seemed to part, and they suddenly found themselves in a low, long room, lined with the black wood of the forest, and at a table at the far end of the warm chamber sat Ned, Cranfallow, and Flewingam. They bolted up, and threw themselves on the companions.

After much back thumping and paw and hand clasping, the friends sat down before the fire to listen to Alane and make their plans.

"Tomorrow, first thing, you must make your way toward Grimm. Your road runs straight and true toward there. I haven't been about for quite some years, but I know our patrols keep the way clear until the end of the Wood."

"Won't we be in danger of being taken again?" asked Bear.

"I think not, Master Bruinlen. Garius won't want to run the risk of having me at his house again. And there is another reason, but we shall pass over that, for it only concerns the welfare of the settlement. I should think the only real danger lies in the bands of the beasts that travel through our lands at times."

"What shall we do for food, my lady?" Dwarf asked, pacing about as he spoke.

"Your provisions are laid out already," replied Alane. "You'll find enough in the pantry to keep you for a while. As for what you shall do for your hunger beyond the Wood, I can't say."

Otter and Bear had opened the pantry door, and were going through the knapsacks of supplies.

"Why, there's enough here to last us for weeks, if we're careful," cried Otter.

"Maybe weeks for you," mumbled Bear, looking woefully at the small packs.

Dwarf walked to the pantry and inspected the stacks of supplies.

"There's enough," he agreed, "if we ration them carefully."

Bear looked hurt, and fumbled through another pack.

"At least there's a little honey," he concluded.

"The water in these parts is good," said Alane, "but once you reach our borders, or on the edge of Grimm, I would be careful what I drank. There were reports from our scouts that the streams in Grimm had been fouled by the beasts. I should take all the good water I could carry if I were to be traveling that way."

Flewingam reached out and touched the old woman's shawl.

"You've been more than kind to us, my lady. We owe our lives to you."

"No such thing," she snapped. "Just saved you a little trouble, that's all."

Alane blushed deeply, and seemed pleased.

"We is both grateful, ma'am, Cranny and I is," said Ned, bowing low.

"I was sure we was to all be digging for the rest of our days, true enough. You has saved us all a powerful lot of grief and sorrow." Cranfallow bowed in his turn.

"But we still needs us a firearm or two," went on Ned. "I doesn't like to think of going through them parts we is gabbing about without no way to take care of my poor old hide."

"I couldn't worry about finding your arms, Master Thinvoice. It seems Hoder has taken a fancy to the weapons he took from you. But I think there are crossbows and shafts somewhere about."

"They'll have to do, Ned," said Dwarf, looking up from a pack.

"Any sort of arms is more than bare-handed," put in Cranfallow, relieved to know they wouldn't be entirely without defense.

"Now I would think you might sleep awhile," said Alane. "There are cots in the other rooms, and supper, if you want it."

"Should we post a guard?" asked Flewingam.

"I shall watch for you," said the old woman.

"You need your rest, my lady," protested Dwarf, but Alane shushed him with a clucking motion of her tongue.

"I am too old to waste my time sleeping," she said. "And I have much to do tonight."

"Then we'll accept your kindness gratefully.

We shall have need of our strength tomorrow."

The small company began preparing for sleep, arranging cots and blankets, and setting out the laden knapsacks within easy reach. Bear and Otter searched until they found the black crossbows and quivers of bolts, and stacked them beside the door.

As the friends settled down in their beds, Otter sat up suddenly, chittering excitedly.

"I'd forgotten all about it, Dwarf. Is the Chest safe?"

"Yes, old fellow," said Dwarf softly, and opening his cloak, he drew forth the tiny box that held the hopes of so many, and the room grew into a glowing river of shimmering gold light that touched their eyes and ears and lifted their spirits as their minds were filled with the wonder and awe of the Arkenchest.

Reassured and strengthened, the companions fell into a sleep of serenity and peace.

Alane kept close watch through the remaining darkness, and prepared for her own rest as the pale trine moon slipped into the first dim light of the awakening day.

And Hoder, with a dozen men, waited impatiently at the gates for dawn, when he knew the ancient woman would find her bed. His dark eyes shone with the glory that would be his, once he possessed the secret powers of the two magicians.

A thin wind began to crawl through the dark trees as the silent band crept near the sleeping ruins of Brosingamene.

A CHIMNEY IN
THE RUINS

Alane dozed fitfully in the carved wooden chair before the dying fire. Faint echoes of memories stirred in her ancient mind, and she watched the flames build and swell into past years, spreading around her until she sat next to Greyfax Grimwald on a faraway afternoon, full of sunlight and gay, white clouds that flew like plumes from the majestic blue crown of the sky. She was young and very beautiful once again, her long brown hair trailing behind her in silken curls and her dark eyes full of the handsome, powerful Elder of the Circle. It was not often such visitors came to the halls of Brosingamene, and although her father had told her of these Masters, she had never dared dream they existed, nor that she would one day stroll in a fragrant garden full of blossoms at the side of one of the most powerful figures in the lower realms of Windameir.

Her new husband, who was growing into the twilight of his life, seemed unimpressed, and even imposed upon, to receive such a guest.

Greyfax had spent only a short time with them, and on the last day, he found her alone, and asked her to walk with him in the broad avenues of the garden. Her young heart had almost failed her, and she was sure he would ask her to go away with him.

But he had spoken to her in a strange voice, and his handsome face had aged. When she looked closely at him in the sunlight, his eyes seemed even older than Lord Brosingamene's, and her spirits fell. It was not until many years later that she recalled his words, after living alone for a very long time in these very ruined walls that had once enclosed that dreamy garden.

He had told her to watch for a dwarf and his companions, and that she must move to aid them. He mentioned Grimm, which even then was but a wasteland, laid bare by the last of the Dragon Wars. And he had said something of an old delving, but she could not remember. Nor could she remember how long she had sought out all the patrols that went into the outer wood daily, but she had eventually given that up and stayed near her hearth fire, growing more convinced with every passing year that nothing would ever come of the wizard's words, and after a span of years, she forgot the warning and took up her studies of the old lore books and spells that had belonged to the First Watcher of Brosingamene. She had been quite alone then, except for the servant her son sent each day with food and drink to sustain her, and, she suspected, to be able to tell Garius when she died.

She felt satisfaction in having outlived that first servant, and now contented herself with seeing the second grow slow of foot and the gray hairs invade his dark head.

When Hoder had begun coming to her dwelling, she had found she had missed contact with the outside world, and welcomed, even anticipated his visits. Through Hoder she learned of the daily raids and forays of strange beast warriors who had grown rife in the outer wood, and of the dwindling defenders, who lost men in almost every skirmish. Hoder was restless and ambitious, and wanted to move the settlement deeper into the old glen, or to leave the forest altogether. He told her he had many men who would follow him, if only he could give them a positive sign that his judgment was right, but so far, he had known no other life but the world of the settlement, and feared they would be lost in so savage a place as the world outside their boundaries.

Hoder had thought to find his omen in Alane.

And she, in her pleasure of his company, had spoken unwisely of many things, and he had found out her secret, that she had borne Garius out of wedlock. When Hoder had told her of the capture of the dwarf, and the werebear and their three companions, the words of Greyfax

had come back to her as clearly as the day he
had spoken them.

And she had made the mistake of saying so
aloud to Hoder.

A flutter of movement startled her from her
reverie, and she jumped, then relaxed again as
she saw the source of the movement was but a
blazing fagot in the fire, falling through the
iron grate. She had begun to doze again when
a faint scraping noise brought her bolt upright
in her chair.

It was the sound of her crossbar being moved
against its lock.

She scuttled to the door with an amazing
speed for bones so old, and firmly latched the
bar, so that it could not be lifted from without.

A disappointed gasp outside told her her
fears had not been misplaced. But she had not
really expected an attempt to force entry to her
dwelling, for even the followers of Hoder be-
lieved her to be a witch, and feared her. Nor
had she expected it quite so soon. Garius would
certainly not risk her displeasure by misplaying
the part he had taken upon himself. It wasn't
that her odd son was not brave, for she knew
him to be a most courageous soldier. It was
only the fear of being discovered to be the son
of a commoner's daughter, and out of wedlock,
that could turn his spirit to water. For the settlement might cast him down if they knew him
not to be of the pure royal Brosingamene line
by both his parents. That thought would stay
his hand, for he would not risk having it spread
abroad, should Alane decide to play her trump

card and wield her secret hold over him in a move to topple his reign. That, of course, was what Garius feared, although Alane had no intention of ever revealing her secret, for it would mean her own end as well.

And knowing Garius would not dare make an attempt to recapture his stolen prisoners would tempt Hoder out into the open, with a clear field to make his own bid for the power he had so long desired.

Alane rightly guessed that her visitors were the objects of Hoder's designs. With such clear proofs that an outside world did in truth exist, and the ruinous knowledge he had of Garius' birth, he could gather even the most reluctant followers to him completely.

There were no windows in the long room, and no entrance other than the thick door. Her house had once been the armory of the great hall, and was unbreachable, except perhaps by siege, but she knew Hoder's plans depended upon speed. She checked the door once more, braced another bar in place, and hurried to wake her sleeping guests.

"What is it?" cried Dwarf as Alane shook him from a light, troubled sleep. He had been dreaming of black darts whistling close to his ear, and awakened to find the noise was Alane whistling through her toothless gums to stir him.

"We must leave now, my little one. We have unwanted visitors."

"Worlughs?" chittered Otter, frantically trying to locate the clumsy, unfamiliar weapons.

"Not beast warriors, if that's what you mean. No, these are far more dangerous. It is Hoder and his ruffians. You would serve his ends nicely, I think."

"But that's one of the soldiers of Garius," blurted out Otter.

"Yes, Master Otter."

"What are we to do?" asked Dwarf, buckling on his pack and arranging the Arkenchest more securely in his cloak. His hand trembled as he held the small object, and the weight of it suddenly almost forced him to sit. He thought of Calix Stay, and safety, but the thought of a journey through more of this wild, savage country engulfed him, and a growing despair settled heavily over his heart.

"I have planned against this day," said Alane in a low voice, excitement running through her words. "We shall go up the chimney flue."

Bear stared at her aghast.

"The chimney!" the companions chorused.

"And a fine chimney it is, with hidden stairs and a passageway into every chamber on every floor. Of course, the top floors are gone now, but I've made the trip myself a dozen times or more. If old knees like mine can climb it, I doubt you'll find it overtiring."

"Do you know how many there are outside?" asked Flewingham, studying one of the crossbows carefully. He fitted a bolt to the weapon as he spoke.

"Only that Hoder does have those bullies he calls his squad. I think a dozen, or more."

"A dozen is too many for the likes of Ned Thinvoice," said Ned.

He stamped a booted foot against the wall.

"I thoughts this was all too soft a road to lasts."

"Bad odds, Ned, but if we can get by without being found out, no harm to us, and no advantage to them."

"You says rightly, Flew. If a Lugh is shooting at you with his gun, and it don't hits nothing, then you ain't hurt, and the Lugh is just one bullet poorer, curse their black souls. But it's bad odds, like you says. And I doesn't take to them things there, with them arrows and all. They isn't what I is used to."

"They'll have to do, Cranny. Our best chance is flight, not fighting. With any luck at all, we'll have need of nothing but our feet," said Flewingam.

"I isn't so sure we has any luck left to us," muttered Cranfallow, and then to himself, "Leastways, not since we has run on you again." He immediately felt ashamed, and went on aloud. "But since we doesn't has no choice, alls we can do is hope them as is after us doesn't has no luck neither."

"Ned, you and Cranny pick up your packs. We must be careful of our food. Flewingam, you and Bear carry the weapons. Otter, I think you'd be of better use in your man form." Dwarf hastily gave his orders and turned to the withered old woman beside him. "I think we are ready, my lady. We must go quickly if we are to put distance between us and our friends outside."

"Then let's be off," spoke Alane, and moving with her crablike gait, she led the comrades into a low doorway that swung mysteriously open when she touched a part of the wall. On the other side, they saw the iron grate where the fire still burned, and smelled the fragrant wood smoke. The passageway was small and cramped, and their eyes were unaccustomed to the thick darkness after looking at the flames. Otter felt the sticky wetness of a cobweb brush his face.

"*Uggh*," he said aloud, startling Bear, who was in front of him.

"What?" called Bear, his voice pinched.

"A spider," replied Otter, hoping the owner of the sticky house was away.

He had had friends who were spiders, but they had always been most polite, and always in a warmly lit corner of his house. It was altogether a different matter to brush against a web in almost total darkness.

His man flesh crawled, and he bumped Bear forward to get away from his unpleasant find.

"Stop pushing," blustered Bear, his voice rising in panic.

"Hush!" warned Alane. "These chimney flues open out aboveground now, and they could hear us."

Bear turned to Otter, and shushed him loudly.

"Griiiibbbbbiiiiitttt," muttered Dwarf, jamming his hat down hard on his head, tempted

to give both his friends a sharp kick in the
shins.

From far away came the distinct murmur of
a whispering voice.

The company fell silent, and strained to
make out the low, hissing sound.

A pebble kicked loose somewhere above
them rattled noisily down the chimney and
landed at Cranfallow's feet.

Before any of them could move, Alane
tugged quickly on Dwarf's cloak and took hold
of his hand. He in turn grasped Flewingam,
who grasped Ned. Thinvoice held to Cranfallow, and on, until the companions grasped hold
of each other in order not to lose themselves in
the pitch darkness of the passageway.

As they moved off, Broco's heart faltered at
the amount of noise they made, but he huffed
up his courage and followed on after the ancient woman.

They seemed to be rising, then Dwarf felt
the steps begin, and they wound their way
sharply upward for a time. The passage seemed
to level, and Alane turned a corner, descended
a few steps, and they found themselves blinking in the sudden light of an open hallway of a
roofless chamber that appeared to have once
been a dining hall.

As their eyes squinted shut from the early
morning sunlight that fell across the broken
hall, Alane leaned near Dwarf's ear and whispered.

"You go on through the hallway until you
reach the garden. It's not hard to find. The old

well still stands, and the outer wall is broken
behind it. You'll find your road beyond."

Dwarf shielded his eyes and looked wildly at
the old woman. He had started to ask how he
could be sure of the way, but she motioned him
to silence with a nod of her head, and continued.

"It is the old Fairlake Road. Follow it as you
can. There will be signs you cannot mistake. It
is all in the manner you are accustomed to, I
think. Some of your ancestors were visitors here
with us awhile. You'll see what I mean. And
now I shall return to play at my favorite game
of hide-and-seek with Hoder. He's not as well
acquainted with my home as I. I shall lure him
off for a while, but go quickly."

Broco turned to thank her, but she wrinkled
her withered old face into a cavernous smile.

"If you see Greyfax ever, tell him Alane has
kept her vow."

Beyond the ruined walls, a quiet footfall was
heard, and without a further glance or word,
the bent figure of Alane had disappeared into
what outwardly looked like sheer stone. A moment later, the sound of what appeared to be
an accidental slip resounded noisily through
the rocks a good distance from where they
stood.

The footfall was distinct this time, running,
and followed by many more. The unseen enemies raced away from them, toward another
part of the Ruins.

Without speaking, the small company made
their way silently through the rock-strewn

room, and quickly passed through the fallen
outer wall.

In the pale halo of light from the new sun,
they saw the weed-grown outline of the road
winding past the broken front gates of the old
halls of Brosingamene, on deeper into the solid
rows of trees that still lingered in shadow.

They quickly tightened their burdens, and
set off at a crouching run toward the silence of
the dark woods, Dwarf in the lead and Otter
bringing up the rear.

They kept casting nervous glances over their
shoulders, but no challenge rang out, and none
of the numbing black darts flew at them from
their invisible foes, and before long, they had
reached the safety of the sheltering trees.

As they stopped to catch their breath, they
heard the high whine of a signal horn, then the
air was shattered with a thin, tearing noise, as
if a strong wind had torn its life on a thorn, followed by a long silence.

"It's Alane," cried Dwarf, beginning to run
toward the sound.

Flewingam caught the little man's arm and
held him behind the trunk of a large tree. "We
can't help her now," he said, cursing.

Broco struggled feebly for a moment more,
then stopped, his body trembling. "Curse their
foul hearts," he moaned, his voice sharp with
fear and anger and grief.

Otter stood, face rumpled in tears of helplessness.

Flewingam patted Broco gently on the shoulder, and had half turned to speak to Otter

when a flurry of dark, ugly bolts rained in upon them.

In the next instant, they saw the running men, led by Hoder, bounding over the fallen garden wall toward them.

TERROR IN THE
WILDERNESS

BROSINGAMENE
ONCE MORE

With a cold, burning flame raging inside him, Broco calmly took a crossbow from Flewingam, and lifted it to his shoulder. He was unaware of his friends calling to him to fly, or the black missiles that flew by his head or struck the earth beside him. All his thoughts were bent upon the green-clad figure racing toward him, and he aimed the unfamiliar weapon carefully, repeating Alane's name as he did so. He cried it aloud as he loosed the bolt at Hoder.

A blazing curtain of violent pain burst over him, and in the brief second of his mind's keenness before the darkness took him, Dwarf saw with sinking heart that the dart had gone wide of its mark.

In the next instant, he was in Flewingam's arms, being carried senselessly away into the deep shadows of the trees.

Bear quickly retraced his steps and helped Flewingam carry Dwarf to safer ground. Ned Thinvoice scrambled back, and crouching low, scooped up the fallen crossbow.

"They're here, men," came the agitated voice of Hoder.

A few angry shouts answered him, and Otter saw the three racing forms in green disappear off to his right, moving to position themselves behind their quarry.

"Quickly, Ned. They've moved to flank us," shouted Otter, and ran toward the others, who were dashing headlong into the ambush.

"Bear," he cried, and motioned with a wildly flying arm to go left.

The companions fled on, Cranfallow leading, veering away from the trap Hoder's men had tried to lay.

Great hanging dead limbs and stunted undergrowth hampered their running, and the sharp bracken and dry gorse pulled and tore at their clothes and flesh. As they moved farther into the closeness of the forest, the thickets grew more impassable, until at last they were forced to go upon hands and knees.

In front of a particularly solid thorn brake, they drew up breathless.

"We can't get through that," groaned Bear, reaching out and touching the wall of thorns.

"I can't hears no one ahind us," puffed Ned, trying to hold his exploding lungs in check.

"They isn't coming from that direction," agreed Cranfallow, his ears straining to pick up the sound of running feet.

"Maybe they knows we is trapped," snapped Ned, the thought draining his already drawn features. "We is in their woods. They knows we can't gets out."

Flewingam shifted Broco's weight on his shoulder, and looked about the dense canyon of trees they had blundered into.

"There's no other way but back, then," he said finally. "We can't go on through this."

Otter stared back down the avenue of thorn brakes and gorse, and his heart felt a leaden tug.

"Let me go back to see where they are."

His face was pale and bleeding from the scratches of the thorns. With a whirling motion, he was once more in his own small gray form, and chittering quickly to reassure his friends, he dashed into the low shadows along the edge of the underbrush and was gone from sight.

Flewingam dared not put Dwarf down, for fear of their being surprised, and they all waited anxiously, scarcely breathing, for Otter's return.

Bear spun his spell, and wiggled his paws and tail to get rid of the fatigue that had come over him in his human form.

"I shall at least make a better show of it in my own hide," he said to himself, unsheathing his gleaming claws and raising himself into fighting position.

Ned let out a startled yelp beside him, in spite of himself.

"I isn't never going to gets used to this," he moaned in a faint voice. "I knows you is with them powers and all, but I swears it scares me plumb out of my boots, it does."

Bear placed a friendly pat on Ned's shoulder.

"I'm sorry, old fellow. I'll try to warn you next time."

Ned's eyes were wide and staring at the great brown paw.

"I is powerful grateful for that," he replied lamely, looking up at Bear's broad muzzle.

Cranfallow hissed them into silence, and tensed, looking away toward the entrance to their dark prison.

The shadows of the trees seemed to loom nearer, and a frail ghost of wind touched the companions' faces, its cold finger making them tremble. Flowing black patterns flickered and faded on the dark earth, and a strange, forlorn wail rode the faint wind.

"Ooooooooohhh, ahhhhhhhh," it called, twice, then three times.

Their hearts stopped at the chilling call.

It came from everywhere at once, and what could have been its echoes came from somewhere beyond the wall of thorns.

Again the lonely horn wept, and the echoes came back, thin, and high, and far away.

As the sad calls faded, footsteps filled the silence, crisp and even, as if someone were marching.

Bear's hackles raised, and he towered up in the beginning of his terrible war dance, eyes blazing, deadly claws and fangs shining with a pale, grim fire.

Ned and Cranfallow dropped to their knees

and aimed their crossbows back along the tree-lined avenue.

Flewingam placed Dwarf behind him and drew his short knife.

"Don't worry," chimed Otter's voice, drowning out their pounding hearts. "It's me."

The companions had seen nothing but the flitting shadows before. Where only thorn and gorse had been now stood a tall, gaunt figure dressed in green and gray, his grave blue eyes studying them intently.

Otter stood beside him, once again in his man form.

"Garius!" chorused the companions.

"I have been careless in my planning," said Garius, not waiting to explain his presence. "I have already told Master Otter how I came to be in these woods so early. Perhaps he can tell you."

Garius fell silent, and looked to Otter.

"Hoder is dead, and all his men with him," blurted Otter. "Garius wasn't in time to save Alane, but he had been following Hoder. He knew there was a plot afoot to overthrow Brosingamene, and that Hoder had been at the root of it all along."

"My mother and I were never close," said Garius grimly, his lips compressed. "But she was very wise, in her own way. When I was younger, I had my own ideas as to how the settlement should be run, which she disagreed with violently, so I banished her to the old hall. In time, the people began rumors about her odd behavior. I let them think what they

would, for I was ashamed and afraid to admit
she was my true mother, and bore me out of
wedlock."

"He wasn't really going to keep us as slaves,"
broke in Otter. "It was a plan he had when he
learned of your capture. He was seeking the
leader of the rebellion against him. He knew
whoever it was would have to use you to draw
the rest of the people into his plan."

"When I was just a young boy, my mother,
Alane, told me of the Master that had visited
Brosingamene. I put it all off to her fantasies, of
course. But when you were brought to me, I realized there was truth to the story. I am not a
learned man in many matters, but I hope I am
at least fair. My mistakes, although grave and
unforgivable, at least were from mere misjudg-
ment, and not an evil turn of mind."

"He didn't have a chance to explain all that
at the settlement," went on Otter. "He was going to free us after he had discovered his traitor."

"And what plans has he now?" asked Flewingam, still unconvinced that their former enemy was in truth in their camp.

"To guide you through my domain, and
provision you with enough supplies to see you
through your journey."

In the excitement, Broco had lain senseless
and overlooked. Otter now gasped, and fell on
his knees at the little man's side. "Fine friends
we make," he lamented. "We've forgotten
Dwarf."

Immediately the comrades were kneeling

beside Broco, feeling about for wounds. Garius bent over the others and examined the motionless form. "I think he has taken one of our stun darts," he said. "Hoder could hardly have risked killing him, or any of you."

He pulled aside Broco's cloak and pointed to a small black dart that protruded below his shoulder.

"Let me nearer there, and we shall have him soon to rights."

The tall figure leaned close to Broco, and after examining him for other hurts, he deftly plucked the dart away.

"He should sleep awhile, but other than that, no harm done. Those bolts are prepared with an herb gathered in our wood here, a secret we have long used in our task of guarding these parts against intruders."

"We can't leave him here," said Bear. "We could at least move him somewhere more comfortable than a bed of thorn growth."

"We shall carry him to my court. It is small amends for so great a wrong, but he shall at least have a proper bed and care."

"I isn't one to hold no grudge, but it seems to me there ain't no sense to that. I has just escaped from there, and now I is to go back on my own two feet?"

Cranfallow looked to Ned for encouragement.

"Cranny has what's in my mind down proper," agreed Ned. "We isn't so bright, but then you doesn't need no mountain of sense to see we is better off than we was."

"I understand your misgivings of me. But I shall try as best I may to show my gratitude for your services."

Bear returned to his man form, and frowned a question to Otter.

"I think for myself, he is honest with us. If he had meant harm, he certainly wouldn't have slain those who were pursuing us."

Otter stood as he spoke, and met the eyes of the companions.

"Then we'll risk it. And no offense, sir. Deeds often speak truer than fine talk."

"Thank you, Master Flewingam. I shall try to redeem myself in your eyes."

The lone, high call of the horn they had heard echoed once more through the wood, and Garius unslung a fine, pearl-colored instrument fashioned in the shape of a winged shell, and blew a quick note that resounded over the Dragur Wood.

It was answered with a brief, fading note, and Garius smiled to himself and replaced the horn in its cover.

"They have found them all. My men shall be here shortly and help you bear your comrade to my halls. And we shall bury my mother where she has dwelled so long, where she belongs. The last mistress of Brosingamene."

A sadness as deep and lasting as the ruins of his once proud home crossed the face of Garius.

"Dwarf would want to be there," said Flewingam, rolling the cloak beneath Broco, forming a pillow for his head.

"I feel it better no mention should be made

of it beyond our circle. Not as yet. There is still a part she can play in flushing out the end of this treason. When the time is ripe, I shall make my peace with the memory of my mother. The sooner she is at her rest, the better. I'm sure your comrade will understand." Garius fell into silence as the movement of many feet announced the arrival of his men.

Appearing from nowhere, the soldiers of Brosingamene stood watching quietly as Bear and Flewingam gently lifted the still body of their friend and began moving after the retreating lord of the strange realm.

Otter and Ned and Cranfallow fell into the procession and walked on beside two men dressed in the same gray and green as Garius until they reached the broken gate of the garden where they had made their escape not an hour before.

An officer approached Garius and pointed without speaking toward a mound of crumbling stones.

Garius nodded, and a detail of men followed him to where the lifeless, ancient corpse of Alane lay, her heart run through with an ugly killing shaft from Hoder's crossbow.

He knelt, lifted her frail body, and carried her to the edge of the old garden, and there laid her down.

Great stones from the Ruins were placed over her, forming a high monument to the last dweller of the ancient halls.

With Alane beneath them, the Ruins lost the last faint trace of life, and the companions were glad to leave the place when at last Garius bowed, kissed the cold stones of his mother's burial mound, and returned to them, his face suddenly older and as craggy and broken as the halls of his blood before him.

The distance to the settlement was not nearly so far as Otter had imagined as he had followed Alane in the darkness the night before, and the group soon reached the court of Garius. They entered the dwelling by a secret route, and came unnoticed into the private chambers of the lord of Brosingamene.

It was as they placed Dwarf on the soft down bed and arranged the coverlets around him that Bear discovered the cloak that had guarded the Arkenchest was empty and the small, bright hope of the war-torn lands of Atlanton Earth was gone.

Bear held the rumpled, travel-worn cloak in unfeeling hands, his eyes wide in disbelief and anger, and the agony of their wasted journey engulfed him, and he lowered his great head to the bed beside Dwarf and wept with bitterness. There had been many deaths this day, and all without even the frailest purpose or meaning.

He was glad Broco was spared the despair and defeat he felt, and he rose without hope to make one last search for the tiny object that carried the strength of the Circle within it, and he prayed with all the fervor of his great heart that somehow, somewhere, those of the Light would be able to help him in this dark hour.

BIARKI, SON OF ALGUNNER

"Where has Bear gotten to?" chirped Otter, walking into the large anteroom that lay outside the chamber where Broco slept.

"He was here a moment ago," answered Flewingam, looking up from the bowl of steaming stew he had sat down to.

"I had a new book I wanted him to read for me. I think it's in his lore."

Otter placed the large, leather-bound volume on the table before him, and began slowly turning the gilt-edged pages.

"There are all sorts of histories here, some I can read, some not. I'm sure this one here is about bears. See?"

He held up the book for Flewingam to see.

On the fine white page, a mighty king glowered out at them, his tall figure clad in brilliant gold and green.

Beneath the intricately designed helmet, the

unmistakable shape of a bear's head showed through.

"I would say it's a bear," agreed Flewingam, his mouth full of the hot soup.

"Let's see that," said Cranfallow, coming around the table to join them. "Well, if I was full of the gourd, I could see that wasn't no man, and I is growing plumb used to the snouts of bears and such."

"Did he say where he was going?"

"He didn't say anything, Otter. He was there helping put Dwarf to bed, and I came out for a bite to eat afterward. I should have thought he would have followed me if he knew there was something to be had for his stomach."

Ned Thinvoice, standing beside the hearth stirring the simmering stew, turned his head to address his friends. "I seen him go out that funny hall we come down. He looked a bit queer, but I puts it all off to a narrow squeak. We is all done in, what with the excitement and all."

"You mean he left again?"

"Right enough, he did. I called out to him to tell him there was grub, but he never heard nothing I said."

Otter closed the book and stood.

"Maybe I'd better go see what he's up to. I don't like the idea of him wandering about alone."

Flewingam met Otter's eye. "Do you think something's amiss?"

"I don't mistrust Garius, if that's what you mean," replied Otter. "It's something I can't quite put my finger on. If there were those that followed Hoder, it wouldn't be logical that they would have all been slain. Once that sort of seed is spread, it is hard to die out."

"Then you don't think Garius has seen the end of his treachery?" Flewingam had put down his spoon, and now screwed his face into a frown.

"Because Hoder is dead? No, I think it likely there is someone who is waiting to take Hoder's place. I think Garius thinks the same. Perhaps there is someone that the faithful Hoder had to trust, who perhaps knew what Hoder knew."

"Then we would still be in danger from him, if he exists."

"And it wouldn't set so well for anyone of that sort to know we were guests of Garius."

Flewingam pushed back his chair and wiped his mouth on his napkin. "Then I'd best go with you."

"I is, too," said Ned.

"No, you and Cranny stay with Dwarf, Ned. I'll feel better if I know he's protected."

"Then that is what we is after, if you thinks it best."

Cranfallow nodded, and entered the room where Broco lay.

"We shall be back soon, Ned. If anything should happen, and we don't return in an hour, tell Garius what has passed."

Ned's eyes grew wide.

"Does you think there's something foul aloose?"

"Not really. I just worry that Bear may be

seen by somebody that needs not know we're
here."

"We isn't much help, but we'll make sure nobody bothers our Dwarf. Poor little blighter, he
was sore upset when them devils slayed that
lady. I was plumb positive he was going to
throw one of them dwarf spells." Ned shook his
head in disappointment. "Them was scary
things I seen him do, but lord amercy, they
sure did make your hair stand up all tickle
like."

"I guess he just didn't have time, Ned," said
Otter.

"I guess not. But sometimes I thinks how
much good scary fun it would be if he was just
to sit down and have a show. Cranny and I has
talked about that. With regular chairs and all,,
and us just sitting there awatching."

"I'm sure he'll do that, Ned, when we reach
the end of our journey."

"Humph," Ned snorted. "I doesn't think we
is ever agoing to get that far. Not in old Ned
Thinvoice's life, nohow."

"We will, Ned," promised Otter.

"Let's see if we can find Bear," he said to
Flewingam. "He may be causing a stir somewhere."

The two friends passed through Broco's
chamber and entered the concealed passageway that led outside the settlement's boundaries.

Far ahead, Bear shuffled back and forth over
the path they had followed back to the hall of

Garius, testing the scent of every clue, but to
no avail.

He went over the Ruins carefully, even
checking the cairn of Alane. He could find no
trace of the lost Chest, and went on dejectedly
toward the open wall and out into the beginning of the dark shadows of the woods.

As he neared the thick wall of thorns and
gorse that had trapped them, an odd spoor
caught his attention. Dark and heavy, it crept
from all directions, and seemed to grow stronger.

It wafted over the heavier, more earthy smell
of the black-trunked trees and the musky smell
of the undergrowth. For the first time since
they had entered the Dragur Wood, Bear had
the definite pleasure of the presence of animals.
And it was not just a random boar, or stag, or
traveling porcupine, or solitary badger.

This spoor was bear.

He cocked his ears back, raised himself on
his hind feet, and mumbled politely the signs
of tree and star, wind and water, and went on
in soft rumbles of his sires and the sires of
them. His growl-snuffle spoke of the illustrious
lore of the hunt, and the thanksgiving, and the
deeper etiquette of asking pardon for trespas-
sing upon another's territory.

He spoke his true secret name, which, of the
companions, only Otter and the wizards and
the lady of Cypher knew.

"I am Biarki, son of Algunner. My home of
old was below the Northern Realms, and be-

yond the mountains of Beginen. My life is
yours."

Bear growled, bowed, and fell silent.

It might be hours before his invisible host
would be satisfied with his discourse and either
offer him acceptance or challenge him to com-
bat.

He sat upon his haunches and turned his
massive reddish-brown head away, as custom
demanded, and resigned himself to wait.

THUMB

▨ "Welcome," boomed a scratchy, low growl, almost before enough time had gone by to begin an acquaintanceship.

Bear's ears shot back, and without thinking, he lowered himself into a defensive stance.

"Our lives are yours," came the stranger's voice.

Bear half raised himself again, and his eyes fell on a medium-sized, inky-black bear, standing before him, bowing low, as was customary between travelers.

"My name is Thumb, and here is Bram, Ham, Lilly, Cress, Elam, Storm, Cryis, and Fornax."

From the darker shadows of the trees crept eight black shapes, each the color of Thumb, and ranging in size from small to almost as large as Bear.

The new arrivals all bowed low, and padded to their places beside their leader.

Bear, as studied in his lore as the next one, knew there were black-coated kinsmen in some unknown place, but he had never, until now, met them in the fur.

He was astounded to the point of almost being rude.

"Well, I never," Bear stammered, then caught himself.

"In the resurrection of Borim Bruinthor," he finished, remembering his manners in time.

"In the resurrection," said Thumb, bowing low once more.

"Is that Borim?" asked the smallest of the black animals.

"Hush, Lilly. Of course it's not. You heard him say his name was Biarki."

Thumb woofed, and cuffed the little animal.

"Lilly is the cub of Ham's old mate," he explained hurriedly to Bear. "She was orphaned after the man beasts killed her mother."

"How long have you dwelled here, Thumb? Have your kind always been in these woods?"

"Not always, brother. My sires came from farther south, from across the Endless Water. I have taken shelter here not for ten turnings."

Bear had fallen easily into the posture of the elder, and questioned the young animals kindly.

"That is a long time in so hostile a home."

"We tried once to escape over Calyon, but the spells we were taught no longer worked. We've found this to be our only safe haven, and even this grows more perilous daily. We have seen three bands of the dark beasts already today."

"Calyon? Is that the River? Calix Stay, I call it."

"It is one, sir. My lore learning came from a very old graymuzzle who wandered in his thoughts."

"And these dark beasts? Are they Mankind, or only partly so?"

"They are of no man realm I ever heard tell of. And they eat raw flesh, and have a hide that's like the ironwood bark."

"Worlughs or Gorgolacs," confirmed Bear, looking about apprehensively.

"They have a regular trail not more than a day from here. There are always some upon it."

"Have you seen any in these parts?"

"Not for some time. The man packs slay them when they come near their shelters. They have slain two of us also."

Thumb's soft woofing had grown lower, and ended on a menacing note.

"I have friends among man," said Bear gently, "and they are brothers as loyal as any I've known. But I have seen the craven heart go about in more forms than simply man."

Fornax, a stout youngster with deep rich fur that was burnished with a lighter gray, rose on his hind legs and bristled. "You may speak lightly of Mankind, but we have sworn our blood oath to slay all of them we can, for Slaner and Dell."

"Hold your tongue, Fornax," growled Thumb.

"I shan't. Nor shall we listen to traitor kind tell us of friends among others than our clan."

Bear nodded his mute agreement, wondering if he would have found himself in his present fix if he had followed the young bear's advice. He recalled well enough he had often thought the same thing since he had begun this seemingly endless journey.

And thinking of that, he remembered what he had come in search of.

"I tend to agree with my young quickpaw, but I think he will find that just as there are the craven-hearted among all kinds, so are there the stouthearted. And I have come in search of a very powerful lore holder that Borim Bruinthor himself once defended."

"The Master?" echoed the black animals, awestricken.

"Yes, my brothers. Borim Bruinthor belonged to the Circle of Elders of Windameir, and rode to battle beside many powerful kings of Mankind when a darkness threatened this Atlanton Earth."

"Don't believe him, Thumb," sneered Fornax. "He's like all the rest. I never heard of the Master dealing with any of Mankind."

"Let him speak, Fornax," cautioned Thumb, his growl low in his throat. The barest show of fangs emphasized his words.

"You are very young, my friend," said Bear gently, "and I can't imagine where you've been reading not to know of Borim Bruinthor's deeds hand in paw with the mighty ones of old who were Mankind. But they are truth, and a dense skull is better mended before it does damage or harm."

Storm, who had moved close behind Thumb, reared upon his haunches and said loudly, "We have no fear of you, stranger. You are large, but we are many."

"And I am also Biarki, descendent of Borim Bruinthor," boomed Bear, and he spun in a cloud of black dust and appeared before the stunned animals in his tall man form. Before they could move to escape or defend themselves, he whirled once more and stood upright, his towering red-brown body overshadowing the cowering Fornax and Storm.

His great voice lifted in a rattling war call, and his deadly fangs and claws flashed a bright fire in the pale sunlight.

Thumb had fallen at Bear's feet, and in a quaking, tremulous voice, pleaded, "Oh, master, spare your poor brothers."

Fornax and Storm had beat a terrified retreat and were nowhere to be seen.

"Stand, Thumb. You have nothing to fear."

The terrified animals peered shyly from between their paws. Lilly quickly ran to Bear and threw her forepaws around his leg in a stout hug.

"Ohh, you're so strong. I'll bet you could cuff Fornax and Storm both without even looking."

"I'll cuff no one, little sister. I have no time to lose. If you all would help me, it would speed my errand. If not, then I bid you good hunting and safe shelter."

"We shall help, if we may," implored Thumb.

"Fornax and Storm shall too, if I have to paw them every step of the way."

"Thank you, brother. But I want no one who has to be beaten into helping. We can get along well enough without them, if need be."

A low commotion in the trees behind them reached their ears, and soon Storm came toward them, shambling in a slow walk, his head hung low.

"It looks as if one of our young hotheads has thought better of it already," said Thumb.

His relief was great. He had no desire to displease such a powerful brother, who had the magic of their lord Borim Bruinthor.

"Then let's be on our way. Least said, soonest mended. I seek a small chest, like so." Bear indicated the size of the tiny Chest. "It is pearl-white, and very powerful. If you find it, call out to me, but whatever you do, don't touch it."

The smaller animals all murmured their understanding, and Bear soon had his party searching about the trail over which they had brought Dwarf earlier.

Flewingam, high in a tree, spied Bear's lumbering, broad back, and dropped a dead branch to let Otter know he had found the object of their search.

And Fornax, savage in his rage at his humiliation, glowered with red, blood-rimmed eyes at the strange, helpless gray animal in the undergrowth a few strides from his hiding place.

GORGOLAC BUGLES

Beyond the great seas of time, Froghorn Fairingay's armies battled an enemy horde for possession of a once beautiful city that was built around a horseshoe-shaped harbor, with high gray cliffs that surrounded the town on every side.

And on the other side of distance, Greyfax led a great war band of silent yellow men through dense green jungles to attack a fortress whose walls were fashioned in the form of giant beasts with long snouts and fierce, projecting tusks. A drenching rain blurred their movements, and the mighty army looked ghostly and unreal in the early gray dawn.

All across the plains of Atlanton Earth, the armies of the Light gathered in a desperate effort to overcome the Dark Queen and her designs to capture the Arkenchest and drown all of the lower creations in her frozen darkness.

And in the depths of the dark wood of the Dragur, Otter cried out in pain and struggled desperately to free himself from the steel jaws of a snarling, vicious adversary.

"Hold, Otter, I'm coming," shouted Flewingam, leaping from branch to branch as he descended the tall tree he had used for an observation post.

Otter, his forepaw numb, snaked around in his loose skin and attached his jaws with all his might onto the drooling jowls of his attacker. The pressure lessened for a brief moment, and he overcame his fear and pain and repeated the old spell Froghorn had taught him so long ago.

Fornax sensed the startling change, and fell back, his blood-filled eyes growing wide in confusion and rage.

His small victim now confronted him in the form of a man, brandishing an evil-looking gleaming thing that he had seen before. It could seek the heart of its foe and slash it, and Fornax did not want to get near its deadly claw.

He bellowed his defiance, bristled once, and lumbered away.

Flewingam rushed up, his dagger drawn.

"Where did he come from?" he panted, then quickly looked at Otter's bleeding arm. "But here, let me bind that arm."

"It's all right, I think. Just bruised and scratched."

"It's a wonder it's not broken, the way that fellow was tossing you around."

"It's sore enough," Otter agreed, "but I think it's in a piece. Did you see Bear?"

"Ahead of us, and following the path beyond the Ruins. Toward the place we met Hoder. There were others with him."

"Whatever could he be doing, I wonder? And who could be with him?"

"Bears, that's who was with him. Of the same kind that attacked you."

"Then we'd best hurry. He may need help."

"It appeared they were following him, rather than pursuing him. They seemed to be searching for something."

A loud woof and answering bark came from the trees ahead of them, followed by low growls.

"I think we've been announced," said Otter uneasily.

"I hope Bear is among better friends than the fellow I met."

"Should I take you back?" asked Flewingam, frowning with concern at Otter's injured arm.

"We haven't time. Bear may need us."

"I don't like it, but as you say, we may be needed. He's off this way."

Flewingam struck out in the direction he had seen Bear follow.

Otter's arm throbbed with the effort of the heavy going, but he clenched his teeth and went on. Thoughts of his own pain were overcome by fear for Bear, and that his big friend might need whatever help he might be able to give.

His vision was blurred from the cold sweat running into his eyes, when Flewingam stopped short on the trail and silenced him with a curt nod.

After a moment, Otter heard the low woofing and snuffling from somewhere nearby.

The two friends drew their daggers and crept carefully on.

Otter heard a sound behind him, and turning quickly to protect his rear, came face to face with his frowning friend.

"Bear!" shouted Otter. "You've given me a fright."

"You've given me one," rumbled Bear. "I thought you were some blackguards from Garius, or worse, a Worlugh war party."

"It's only Flewingam and myself. We got worried about you when you disappeared."

Flewingam came marching toward them, his features drawn, escorted on both sides by Bear's stout black friends.

"Ah, well met, Flewingam. I see you've met my companions."

Upon seeing his friend, and fearing no further harm from his guardians, Flewingam launched into the near tragedy Otter had suffered in the renegade's attack on him.

Thumb listened gravely, his muzzle growing more grizzled as the story went on to its climax.

"I've been worried for some time about Fornax," he said, as Flewingam drew his tale to a close. "I had thought his hot temper only natural, for he lost two kindred to the Mankind beyond the old river settlement. And his sire was slain by the beasts with yellow eyes who roam these hunting trails now. But I did not think he would go bad. I've been able to reason with him before."

Otter, to the amazement of Bear's new friends, repeated his spell and returned to the more comfortable form of his true shape.

He carefully inspected his mauled forepaw.

"I can well understand his anger at Mankind," he said softly, chittering in pain, then wrinkling his whiskers. "But there is an unwritten code among our kindred souls about needless slaying. And bears and waterfolk have long been friends of old."

Lilly recovered from the speechlessness and shock first, and loped to Otter. "Ohhh," she cooed, rumbling a deep, purring sound far inside her throat. "Look, Thumb. I've only heard stories of his kind. Why, he's so snuggly."

She grasped Otter roughly, making him cry out in pain and surprise.

"Lilly," cried Thumb, leaping to remove the struggling animal from her stout squeeze.

She dropped him suddenly, and Otter's ears were wrinkled and fussed, and his whiskers bent.

"Phhheeeew," he gasped. "I'm sure the pleasure is mine," he managed.

"He's so warm and squeezable," moaned Lilly, "and so tiny. Why, I could carry him about all day long and not even know it."

"If you don't mind," murmured Otter, backing away from his new admirer.

"You'll have to forgive her, brother. She's never come upon many different animal clans. She's only been away from her sow for a few months."

"May I keep him, Thumb? For my very own?"

Otter emitted a low whine.

"No, Lilly. You do not keep brothers."

"Then aren't we keeping Biarki?" asked the young she-bear.

"Of course not."

Thumb shuffled his forepaws in embarrassment.

Flewingam interrupted sharply.

"I find your company most delightful, and am deeply honored by your friendship, but my friend Bear, I fear, is going to tell us now what errand he was upon to bring him this way."

Bear slumped down in a dejected pose, his great head hung low.

"I came in search of the Chest," he blurted out. "When I went to fold Dwarf's cape, it was gone. I knew he always kept it there. I thought it might have been lost along the way somewhere."

Otter and Flewingam gasped, sitting down beside Bear.

"You mean it's lost again?" wailed Otter, a double despair settling over his heart.

"I've searched everywhere, but to no avail," moaned Bear.

"Did you see signs of anyone else being

here?" Flewingam's voice was tight, and he looked at the ground as he spoke.

"There was no one about but us," said Thumb, confused and upset by his new companion's sorrow.

"Could it have been one of the men who carried Dwarf?"

"No, Otter. I carried him most of the way, and I didn't take my eyes off any of them until we had Broco safe in the room."

"Then perhaps it's in his room?"

Bear's head shot up, his hopes returning.

"I didn't search the room," he said, a faint trace of cheer creeping over his broad muzzle.

"Then that's where it must be," chittered Otter. "It's probably fallen under the bed."

"Let's hurry back and see."

"I think you've probably hit upon it, Otter. It must have fallen out somewhere in the room. If it's not here, and no one else has found it, then it must be in Broco's room."

Flewingam stood, and helped Otter up.

Bear lumbered over to Thumb, and the two carried on a lengthy conference, of which Otter and Flewingam could understand nothing. Whistling grunts and growly wheezings, followed by woofing coughs, were all that met their ears, and at last, Bear stood high on his hind legs and made an odd sign to Thumb, who repeated the ritual.

The circle of black animals then all coughed and growl-barked twice, and the meeting seemed to be over.

"I hope the Chest is safe in Dwarf's room,"

said Otter, aside to Flewingam. "I hate to think all we've gone through is wasted."

"It will be there, safe and sound," replied his friend, trying to make his voice sound more certain than he felt. A dark shadow of fear had crept near his heart, and he felt its presence like the cold hand of Dorini closing over his mind. He struggled momentarily with the terror, then thrust it out into the light. "It will be there," he said aloud, to shake off the last lingering doubt.

Bear shuffled to them and answered their questions of what had been said in the odd meeting.

"They are sheltering not far from here, near where the settlement of the river men lay. They have offered us aid, should we need it."

"They are always a welcome ally," said Otter, bowing to their new friends.

"And they have offered to guide us through Grimm."

"Dwarf will be pleased to hear of that. Do they know the place well?"

"They traveled, or at least Thumb and Cryis did, through there long ago, in search of food and shelter. It doesn't sound very inviting, but there is meager food and drink there, if you know where to look. Or there was, the last time they had need to venture there."

"Then let's hurry," chirped Otter. "Maybe Dwarf will be awake, and we can tell him this gladdening news."

"And search for the Chest, as well."

No one mentioned what lay in store if the

Arkenchest were indeed lost. They filled their
thoughts instead with the welcome promise of
having their way shown across Grimm, and of
the safety that lay across Calix Stay.

As they started back down the avenue of
trees toward the halls of Garius, a faint,
faraway alarm horn called high and long, answered by dim man shouts, and over the horns
of Garius bleated the ugly voices of Gorgolac
bugles, ringing harsh and keen on the afternoon wind.

NED THINVOICE
MENDS A CLOAK

Ned Thinvoice sat beside Dwarf's bed, bent over the work of mending Broco's torn cloak.

He paused, thread between his teeth.

"What does you make of this, Cranny?" he asked, holding up a small object that had fallen from the rip he was trying to repair.

Cranfallow crossed the room and took the tiny Chest in his hand.

"Some trinket of our Dwarf's, I expects. Him with his powers and all, it might be a wizard's snuffbox. We had best leaves it lay."

"Well, I wasn't snooping none. It plunked itself out of his cloak while I was amending it," snapped Ned, more uneasy than angry, thinking of the results if it was indeed a dwarf witch's trinket.

"Puts it back where you found it, Ned. We has enough troubles as we is."

"You isn't telling no lies there," said Ned,

putting the small Chest back inside the cloak
and stitching it fast inside.

Cranfallow stooped beside Dwarf and arranged the blankets over the little man.

"I doesn't like this. First we is hog-tied and
throwed in a hoosegow, then we is the best of
friends. Something just ain't quite straight,
Ned."

Thinvoice stopped his sewing and furrowed
his brow.

"Then you says the same as I, Cranny. I
hasn't had no queer feeling like this since afore
Seven Hills."

A noise in the outer chamber startled the
friends, and they fell into silence, listening with
held breath.

Ned Thinvoice sprang up in alarm at the
sudden knock on the door.

Without waiting for a reply, Garius Brosingamene strode into the room, carrying a small silver tray.

Cranfallow's hand flickered toward the hilt
of his dagger, while Ned moved to the front of
Broco's bed.

"Ah, good Cranfallow. Thinvoice. I've brought
a potion that should have our friend as good as
new in a short time."

Cranfallow peered cautiously at the contents
of the silver tray.

"What's it for?" he asked abruptly.

"It's the remedy for the stun dart. Merely
herbs and barks. A simple potion to offset the
effects of sleep."

"I doesn't know about that sort of goings-on

none. We'll waits until our friends gets back afore we give our Dwarf no sorts of them potions."

Garius put the tray down on a small table at the foot of the bed.

"As you wish."

His cold blue eyes fell on Cranfallow, forcing him to lower his eyes.

"You don't trust me yet, do you, Master Cranfallow?"

"It ain't that, sir. It's just we doesn't knows about medicines and such, and we'll just holds off a bit, until we hears what Flew, or Otter, or Bear says."

"And where have they gotten to?"

Garius' voice lowered, and his hard blue eyes darkened.

"They has stepped out for a bit of air, they has," Ned quickly replied, looking warningly at Cranfallow.

Garius seemed to stare off into space a moment, then, as if thinking aloud, he muttered, "I hope they haven't come to mischief. It wouldn't do for anyone to find out they're here."

"They isn't abroad on no pleasure outing," said Ned shortly, then bit his lip. "I means they ain't going to be seen by nobody, nohow."

"I hope not, Ned. It might yet go ill for us if certain parties were to know Hoder has been slain. Or that the objects of his game were safe within my walls."

"Then why is we here?" asked Cranfallow. "I means aside from our Dwarf being hurt, and all. We could just as easy hole up in the woods. We has done it enough times afore now."

Garius smiled faintly.

"The play hasn't seen the last act, Master Cranfallow. It has cost my poor mother her life, and brought a once trusted man to his doom. But there is yet another scene to come."

"What else is there that ain't been run out? Hasn't you found your two-tongue?"

"Only one, good Ned. There was more afoot than I bargained for, it seems. But we shall have the lot of them." Garius paused briefly, frowning. "If our friends aren't discovered."

"They hasn't strayed none," said Ned reassuringly. "Why, they is probably on their way back now."

"I'll go sees if I can roust them," offered Cranfallow, starting for the door.

"Did they go back out the hidden entrance? Then I'll go myself. I think I know the way better than either of you. Stay and tend your friend. I'll only be a moment."

Before Ned or Cranfallow could protest, Garius had disappeared into the concealed entryway and was gone.

"Now what does you make of that bean stew?" said Ned. "First he says we isn't welcome, then he's all aflap cause some of us is gone."

"I can't makes him out. But I hopes Flew and Otter and Bear is on their way back."

"Do you reckon we should gives our Dwarf a little of his brew?"

"Not yet, anyhows, Ned. We just sits tight, I says, to see what we'll see."

"And what do you make of all that fancy talk about plays and such? 'We hasn't seen the last scene yet,' he says."

"Most likely the way them fellows talk. I wouldn't hold no store by it."

"I wouldn't hold no store by it if we was safe somewhere else, with as many miles atween us as our poor old foots would carry us."

Garius reappeared through the hidden doorway as Ned fell silent.

"They were nowhere about. Are you sure they went out this way?"

"As sure as you is standing there, sir. I seen 'em go, first Bear, then Otter and Flew. I thoughts it were odd."

"What was odd?"

Ned smiled shyly, and looked down as he spoke. "Well, sir, Bear. We was cooking up a stew, and him being big and all, and you know how big ones does has a hunger on 'em all the time. But he went prancing off without even so much as a sniff at the mush."

"That does seem odd, Ned. Was there anything bothering him?"

"I couldn't say rightly, sir," said Ned, once more careful of his words, and fearing that he had already said too much. "He seemed kind of upset. But then we was all afeeling that, what with a narrow squeak like we had, and all."

Garius paced a few worried steps, his eyes narrow blue slits. A clouded expression played over his face, and he spoke so suddenly it

startled Ned into dropping the cloak he had
been holding as they talked.

"I'd best send one of my men to find them.
They've probably lost the way. This entrance
can be hard to find from outside."

And saying no more, he left the two friends
staring dumbfounded at the door as it closed
behind him.

THREE IN A TUNNEL

▧ "Well, blow out my torches," began Ned, but was interrupted by the arrival of a somber stranger, dressed in the uniform of Garius.

He was tall and thin, and wore a dark green cap on his head, and carried an ugly black crossbow, and a dozen or more of the short stun darts in a quiver at his belt.

Cranfallow stepped forward to speak, but the gaunt figure crossed the room and closed the door behind him, never once looking at either of the friends.

"There goes a rude 'un. Never so much as a howdy-do."

Cranfallow quickly opened the secret entrance and followed along after the vanished man a few steps.

"He's gone clean," reported Cranfallow, poking his head around the door.

"Not far enough for my likings," sneered Ned,

picking up the cloak and spreading it out on his lap.

"Well, get on with your mending, Ned. I'll stand watch here awhiles, just so's nobody will come asneaking back down this hole without us on to 'em."

Ned Thinvoice had found his needle and thread, and sitting beside Dwarf, bent to his work once more.

A faint, faraway horn call caused him to prick himself badly, and as he put the injured finger to his mouth, he heard another, closer still, and out of the middle of the strange camp, he heard the answering calls. With pounding heart and fallen hopes, he strained to hear what the men were shouting. And the terrifying answer rang back, harsh and guttural, filling the room with the dreadful, ugly wail of Gorgolac war horns.

Cranfallow bolted through the hidden entrance, his pale face haggard, the short dagger in his hand.

"Them won't be no use against them Lacs. What'll we do, Cranny?" cried Ned.

"Get him up. We'll gets him out of here, leastways."

Shots and cries rang throughout the camp, and nearer, in the very hallway beyond, they heard rifle shots, and screams.

"Come on, Ned. Grab him up. We'll sees if we can hide in here."

Thinvoice wrapped Dwarf in his cloak and slung the little man over his shoulder.

"Gets on with it," shouted Ned. "They has set the hall afire."

Stumbling and half crouched, the two, Ned with Broco over his shoulder, made their way into the gathering gloom of the passageway.

Pausing to shift the weight on his back, Ned looked back. He sniffed the air, and turned back to Cranny.

"They has set us afire. Them roofs is just like tinder. And them crossbows ain't got a chance against them rifles."

"It don't look so good," agreed Cranfallow, breathing hard, "but we has to gets out of here. We'll gets on, and maybe we'll find the rest of our bunch. They has to be somewheres out here."

"If them Lacs ain't found 'em first," said Ned grimly. He patted the senseless Dwarf on a pointed-toed boot. "Seems likely our luck is always afoul whenever we has our dwarf witch with us."

"As likely as our luck is afoul as when you is gabbing about them things that is better left as they lays. Now move them knobby knees of yours if you wants to see the right side of your supper dish."

Ned laughed bitterly. "We *is* most likely supper, if them Lacs has their way."

A figure sprinted down the dim passageway toward them, and Cranfallow braced himself, holding the short dagger before him.

The thin figure of the soldier Garius had sent loomed into the light. He drew up breathlessly. "Where is Garius?"

"Couldn't rightly say, friend. Them Lacs has set the place afire. We is trying to get ourselves as far away as we can. You'd best be looking to your own feet."

Ned jerked a thumb in the direction the man had just come. "Is they any way out there?"

The green-clad figure hesitated, looking back down the passage toward the room where Broco had been placed.

Making a decision, he sighed, and turned to Cranfallow. "Up ahead you'll find the opening clear. You can find your own way then."

"What is you about?"

"I have to return to Garius."

"That's plumb crazy, friend. They is inside the camp," said Ned.

"All the more reason."

The man bent his crossbow and loaded it, and without speaking further, he raced on toward the flames that were now visible to the two friends. In another moment he was lost in dirty blackish-gray smoke.

The rifle shots had ceased, but the noise of the fire grew louder. Broco groaned, and shifted feebly on Ned's back.

"I think he's coming around. We better move on," said Ned, his eyes watery from the smoke, and his voice pinched.

They found the passage door choked with smoke, but after Cranfallow scouted ahead, he motioned Ned that it was clear of the enemy. A moment later, they were outside, taking great gulps of the fresh late afternoon air. After they caught their breath, they carefully studied their surroundings.

Behind them, the settlement of Garius was in flames, with thick, billowing columns of iron-colored smoke rising above the burned shells of houses.

Only an occasional shot broke the grim silence, and over the crackling roar of the fires, loud shouts and curses rang out, all in the guttural rasp of the Gorgolac tongue.

"I think we has seen an end of them strange men," said Cranfallow, shaking his head. "They wasn't the best of sorts, but they was men."

"What is we agoing to do now?" asked Ned, bent over with the weight of Dwarf. "We can't sits here saying no last words for them poor beggars."

"Let's go on back to where we was. To Alane's house. That may be where our fellows has gotten to."

And so saying, Cranfallow took the lead and headed back in the direction of the Ruins of the old halls of Brosingamene. Looking over his shoulder every few steps, Ned hurried on after him. Soon the rusty gray Ruins were before them, and they stopped to rest once more, and Cranfallow took his turn at carrying Broco.

Cranfallow looked about him, a resigned frown on his face. "This here is ruins, and the last person dead and buried this morning."

Looking back toward the reddish-black pillars of smoke, he added, "And this afternoon, all them folks back there is had up by that bunch of Lac filth, and now they ain't no more left." He shook his head dazedly. "We is lost, and they ain't no way we can go that ain't brim full of some sort of mischief that is like to be the death of our own selfs."

"We might make a start by putting me on my own two feet," broke in Dwarf huffily, kicking Cranfallow feebly in the chest.

"Why, bless me, our Dwarf is come out of his fit," said Ned, helping Cranny set the small form carefully down.

Broco blustered weakly, and straightened his hat. He paled when he felt for his cloak, but regained his color when Ned draped it about his shoulders.

"I was going to mend up them rips, but I didn't get through afore them Lacs come on us like they done."

Ned shuffled his feet and looked at the ground. To his surprise, Dwarf didn't conjure any spells out of his hat or berate him at all. Instead, he looked about in confusion, and at last turned to his friends, his eyes somehow not quite in focus.

"Gorgolacs?"

"But then you has had a nice nap, too."

Cranfallow clicked his tongue at himself, and quickly filled in the broken parts of the story for Broco, from the happenings of the morning, and the burial of Alane, and Garius taking them in, and Hoder's death, and Bear, Otter, and Flewingam's disappearance. Dwarf listened attentively, and when Cranfallow at last drew his tale to a close, he paced back and forth restlessly, piecing together the happenings in his mind and trying to decide what best to do.

Ned and Cranny waited in silence, looking from Broco to the tall, thinning columns of smoke behind them, and glancing nervously at the gathering afternoon shadows in the forest beyond the Ruins.

"We can't stay, and we don't dare go on, for fear of losing our companions," he said at last. "Do we have arms?"

"Nothing but this butter knife," spat Cranfallow, patting the hilt of his short dagger.

Dwarf turned and stared away in the direction of the smoldering settlement. A dark pall hung heavily over the sky in that direction, and Broco's brow knitted. Almost as if he'd willed it, a cool wind sprang up from the east, and low-flying rain clouds crawled slowly over the darkened tops of the woods and a steady downpour dimmed the edges of the sky.

"Our course lies in the road Alane gave us, before Hoder put his hand to it. Perhaps we'll find our friends there before us."

"If they is to be found at all," grumbled Ned dejectedly.

Dwarf looked up at his companion and gave him a hearty thwack on his backside.

"Good heart, Ned, that's what we need. And a good walk will clear these spider's nests out from between my ears."

Broco gave a forced laugh and set out at a brisk pace, trying not to think of the possibility of their friends not being at Alane's home before them.

As they neared the crumbling stones that were Alane's home, Dwarf's face brightened. "We'll look to ourselves here. Perhaps we can find stores and arms, as well as our friends."

Ned and Cranfallow cheered visibly at the mention of arms and meeting with their lost comrades, and the three set off rapidly to seek what the ancient halls of Brosingamene had left to offer.

Far behind them, Flewingham, Bear, and Otter crouched beside Thumb and his band, and watched in growing horror as the grisly Gorgolac warriors set to their horrible feast.

They had seen no survivors of the realm of Garius Brosingamene, Tenth Watcher of Amarigin.

The companions turned away in sickened revulsion and with fallen hearts, and set off quietly toward the sheltering depths of the woods. Bear and Otter wept openly, and Flewingam swore horrible oaths under his breath, and none of the three mentioned a word about what might have been the fate of their friends, trapped in the deadly walls of the flaming camp.

FORNAX

▩ Bear and Flewingam sat heavily down beneath a thorn brake, while Thumb lined up his group to count noses after their dash for the safety of the woods.

Otter stared back along the line of trees that sheltered them from the gutted settlement. His tiny paws were clenched, and his gray body moved to and fro in silent, unvoiced agony.

After a moment more of this unbearable anguish, he turned, and with a choked voice, spoke. "I won't believe they're gone until we can check the hall."

Holding to that small, slim hope, his voice became more sure. "And there's nothing left for us without Dwarf, Ned, and Cranny. If the Chest is lost, or worse, taken, then we may as well end it in a stand over our comrades' graves."

He turned his head again in the direction of the burning settlement.

"If only Greyfax or Froghorn were here," he went on wistfully, half aloud.

Flewingam was the first to shake off his stunned disbelief. He rose and went to stand beside Otter.

"We have no weapons for a fight, old friend, although I stand with you on the matter of a search. We'll wait here until those foul things have done with their ugly feast."

Bear, his head between his two huge paws, raised a stricken whisper that bordered on a wail. "Surely they must have escaped. They must have gotten out the secret entrance. We can't have come all this way just to end like this."

"There is a good chance they did escape, brother," put in Thumb, lumbering to his large friend. "They have many caves in that man camp. We've lived in these woods for some time now, and we've often come across tunnels and such they have dug. Nothing near as good or smooth or fine as a bear makes, but holes, nonetheless. And they show up in all manner of places. We can check them, if you like."

Bear woofed once, and his great frame straightened a bit. He talked to Thumb in their own tongue a moment, then turned to Otter and Flewingam.

"Thumb has given good advice, I think. He says you and Flewingam should go with him, and I'll take his bunch, and we'll complete a search of all the tunnels out of the settlement.

We'll have to wait until morning, but in the meantime, we'll make for the Ruins of Alane. Our work can start there, at dawn, and we can meet there again at dark."

The friends, glad of any plan that would keep their thoughts from what they feared most—not finding their lost companions, or worse still, finding only their remains in the settlement—hastily agreed, and the troop set out through the twilight toward the old Ruins of Alane, with Thumb leading and the rest of the small company following cautiously behind. Bear brought up the rear, glancing over his shoulder at every step.

They had not gone far when they discovered the mortally wounded Fornax, half hidden beneath the foul-smelling carcass of a slain Gorgolac. Thumb called out in dismay and loped to his fallen brother. Woofing, and rumbling low in his throat, he danced the ancient rites of Beardom around the doomed Fornax, bowing and shuffling, raising and lowering his head in time to the odd music that ran endlessly through his blood. Bear and the others joined in and soon all the animals were swaying in a circle around the dying animal. Otter chittered and whistled in low, mournful calls, and Flewingam bowed his head at the strange, moving sight before him.

Their mourning over, Thumb quickly moved close to the fallen bear and placed his muzzle to the dying Fornax's ear. He spoke quickly, then leaned closer to hear his friend's reply. He stayed in that position for a great while, rum-

bling now and again, as if assuring Fornax he
had heard something that was said, or agreeing
with some thought or other.

It was an hour past sunset when Thumb
sighed deeply, growled, lowered his head
twice, and moved his paws in a circular motion
over the still, cold form of Fornax.

"He's gone," said Bear to Otter, without looking away from the shadow of Thumb outlined
against the darker forms of the trees beyond.

"Wasn't that the one who attacked you, Otter?" asked Flewingam in a low voice.

"Yes," answered Otter simply. "But I wouldn't
have wished the fellow harm."

"He was an unhappy sort," agreed Bear,
"and from what he was saying to Thumb, I
gather he had discovered the Gorgolacs and
was trying to get warning to his band."

"Why the sudden change of heart?" asked
Flewingam, a trace of disbelief lingering in his
tone.

Bear looked at Flewingam for a moment, his
deep brown eyes growing misty, woven with
the most ancient signs of Beardom, of the lines
of the great King Bruinthor, and the timeless
kinship of all life.

"There was no change of heart, old fellow,"
said Bear sadly. "He was hotheaded, and perhaps misguided. But for all that, he was, after
all, still a bear."

Lilly, aided by the others, placed branches of
thorn over Fornax, and Thumb patted the lifeless animal twice, and turned back to Bear.

"He said he saw men come out of one of the

tunnels near here, making for the old man shelter."

"Then they did escape," cried Otter, dancing a small jig at Bear's feet.

"But he said nothing of your friend, the small one," went on Thumb. "I'm sure he would have mentioned seeing a halfman."

Otter stopped in mid-step, and his brow furrowed. "Perhaps he didn't notice," he said hopefully. "Dwarf can be very cautious when he wants. Almost as good as an animal when it comes to hiding or going about unnoticed."

Thumb looked down sadly at the small gray creature. "It's possible he didn't see your friend. As you say, he might not have noticed anything more because of the man-beast attack."

"And there's Ned and Cranny. We left them with Dwarf. I know they're not the sort of comrades that would leave a friend in a pinch." Bear gave Otter a reassuring pat.

"I'd forgotten that," said Otter, looking up at his friend. "Of course. Old Ned and Cranny would have found a way out, if one was to be had."

Thumb stepped forward, and lowered his voice to a whisper. "If I might suggest silence, we can get on with our plans. And there are still those ugly things about."

They had all forgotten the presence of the enemy troops in the heartening news Fornax had given, and they now looked warily about them and drew further into the dark eaves of the forest.

Bear addressed Thumb as the companions quietened. "Can you lead us to the old man shelter in the dark?"

"As easily as by daylight. And there will be less chance of being seen by those others." Thumb jabbed a paw in the direction of the blood-red glow of the waning fires that burned sullenly behind them.

"Good. Then we'll press on until the Ruins, and see what's to be done then. With any sort of luck at all, our friends will be there before us." He paused and looked questioningly at Flewingam and Otter. "If not, we'll see in the morning."

Bear quickly turned away so his companions could not see the cloud of misgivings that had crept into his eyes.

Thumb gathered his small band and gave a low, chuckling rumble to signal he was ready.

Bear, Otter, and Flewingam pushed away the dark thoughts that troubled them, and glad of the business at hand, set grimly off into the chilling blanket of darkness that had fallen over the hostile woods.

SECRETS OF THE EARTH

UNEXPECTED COMPANY

⬚ "It won't do," said Dwarf shortly, dusting himself off as he emerged from the hole among the Ruins. "I can't find the infernal door without a light. All of these entries look the same in the dark. We could be here past doomsday, at this rate."

"Then we oughts to hole up somewheres and waits for daybreak."

Cranfallow grunted his agreement.

"I hate to think of sleep without something on my stomach, but I'll guess we shall have to wait," said Broco, trying to ignore his hunger and thirst.

His head throbbed painfully, and his throat was choked with the stone dust he had disturbed in the musty Ruins.

"Well, we isn't so bad off as them others. We can still talks about supper, instead of ending up in the stewpot for them Lacs, leastways."

Dwarf let out a coughing, dark laugh. "That's a matter of opinion, good Ned. I'm sure those louts would disagree with that. Although they might find dwarf stew a bit tough and chewy for their likes."

"Well, they has a fire and full bellies, curse their filthy hides. But I don't knows if I would swap boots with their nasty selfs, for all that."

"We'll find the opening tomorrow, Ned. I'm sure I can find it with daylight. Then we'll have a late breakfast, and a nap, and make what plans we may. And by then, the others will have probably found their way here."

Cranfallow's hand touched Dwarf's shoulder in a motion for silence. Broco started to blurt out a question, but the distinct sound of movement somewhere nearby kept him silent, and they strained to hear what new danger was upon them.

"It ain't no Lac," whispered Ned, breathing the words at Dwarf's ear. "Too quiet for the likes of them."

Almost silent footsteps stealthily drew up, then resumed their way. A small ching of metal against stone followed, and the steps ceased. Another noise, of earth being moved, as if someone were digging, reached their ears. The three friends sought this new intruder through the heavy cloak of darkness, so deep and black no stars shone through. A tiny glimmer of dim, reddish light flickered over the trees, but it was so faint and far away, it seemed only a trick of the eyes. In the silence, the quiet movements came like avalanches of sound.

Cranfallow eased his short dagger out, and Ned's hand curled around a fist-sized rock. Under his cloak, Broco grasped the small Chest in one hand, and the other grasped the dragon stone that Bear had returned to him in Cypher. And as he remembered Cypher, his heart lightened and his fear abated.

He touched his hat with a rapid motion of his hand, and a small hum began, barely audible at first, then growing until it seemed to come from the very rocks themselves. Pale golden light crept over the darkness like liquid fire, and touched the tumbled brow of the Ruins, making wild shadows flicker and turn on the ancient, fallen halls.

"Lordy be," breathed Ned through clenched teeth. "He's gone and worked up one of them spells." A thin tremor of excitement ran through him, making him forget his fear.

Cranfallow cast a worried glance in Dwarf's direction, but saw nothing but the glimmering outline of his hat. His attention was pulled once more to the Ruins, now swimming in a soft silver beam of light, and there amid the fallen pillars and archways stood Garius Brosingamene, struck silent and motionless in the ghostly sea of burnished silver darkness.

"Well, strike my colors if it ain't old Brozy hisself," said Ned, his eyes wide in wonder, more at the dwarf's magic than at the man he now saw standing before them.

"Garius!" called Broco, and as he spoke, the pale light flared and vanished.

The sudden darkness was blinding, and Garius let out a small cry, falling as he tried to back away from the enchanted voice.

"Garius," called Dwarf again, "it's Broco, Dwarflord, and two friends. We mean you no harm."

A scraping sound followed by halting footsteps reached the companions, and the dim outline of Garius appeared before them.

"Is that you, Master Dwarf?" asked the shaken voice of the still stunned heir of the ill-fated halls.

"Myself, and two comrades. We made good our escape from the attack through your tunnel."

"The same as I," said Garius tiredly. "But I'm afraid the others did not fare as well. This day has seen the end of the Watchers of Amarigin. My family is gone, and all the rest as well." Garius laughed bitterly and sat down. "All the schemes and counterschemes have found their end in a roasting pit. My hand was underplayed, and the other traitor has turned the likes of that beast filth on us by betraying the border guards. And now all is quits." He turned to Broco. "No offense, sir, but it seems you have brought no good luck to my realms."

"It was no ill luck of my own making," huffed Dwarf. Then, going on in a gentler voice, he added, "But you are welcome to join us. There is no sense in your staying on here now. We're making for the River, and beyond. We have powerful friends there who can help us, if we can win through to them."

"The Watchers never leave, except by the

grave," said Garius grimly. "And my grave has already been dug here."

"As you will," said Dwarf. "But can you find the entry into the Ruins? Were you going there when we found you?"

"Yes," confessed Garius, "I was going there. The vaults of my fathers still lie beneath the ruins."

"Can you find Alane's old quarters?"

"I'd be a fool if I couldn't. Yes, I'm quite familiar with my mother's house. Come."

Rising, Garius stumbled and fell, and did not stir himself.

Ned was at his side first, and he held up a bloody hand to his friends as they knelt beside the fallen king.

"He's taken a sore wound," said Ned grimly. "They has shot away his insides."

Dwarf leaned close to the wounded man's face. "Can you show us the doorway?" he asked softly.

"The blue stone," muttered Garius, "blue stone . . ." His blanched face seemed to darken, and his eyes fluttered weakly. "The vaults," he gasped. "The vaults . . . of Brosingamene below . . . armory."

Garius breathed heavily, choking for breath. "And I have to make a clean chest of myself, sir, or I shall not rest easy. If you will give me your word that you will place me in my vault, with the other Watchers, I will tell you all."

His agonized glance fell heavily upon Dwarf.

"We shall see to it," assured Broco. "Rest easy."

The gaunt figure tensed once, as if in pain, and spoke in a softer tone. "Good. I knew I could count on you. It was this way. My mother told me of the wizard's visit, and of the dwarf that would come. It would be an omen that would mean the end of the line of Brosingamene. It was a curse put on us by those miserable ancestors of yours that we slew so long ago, when we caught them crossing our borders. They said Brosingamene would fall at the hand of one of their kind. I thought Alane daft, until you showed up. Alane and I devised a scheme whereby the signs would not be met. And we also planned to smoke out our traitor."

Garius coughed, and his body was wracked with a shuddering tremor.

"And now I see that it all fell out as it was fated." He half laughed, then coughed again. "We had it from an outguard that one of the man-beasts who was slain when you were captured had tried to save his hide and had done some bit of talking, trying to make a deal to save his life."

"Tried to make a deal with who?" broke in Dwarf, trying to comfort the dying man by putting a rolled cloak beneath his head.

"Jokim," spat Garius, "my trusted Jokim. It was a movement within my own guard that plotted to overthrow me and move the settlement beyond the Wood. And Hoder was but a small fish, and expendable. But the catch of it all was to have you. The half beast spoke of a runtling, and that his overlord was most interested in runtlings. And for any who brought

him a runtling who traveled with animals was
the choice prize. It meant unlimited power, and
an army to command, and booty."

Garius groaned, and a small trickle of blood
crept over the corner of his lips.

"I must hurry. Listen well," Garius gasped.
"I have no forgiveness to ask. You were a threat
to my own kingdom and people. I had thoughts
that if I somehow could trick Hoder or his su-
perior into moving, they would take you from
Alane. I gave no fight that night, so that it
would make it easier for Hoder and his men.
Especially if they thought I was afraid of making my mother angry. Then when they failed, I
hoped to lure whoever else was behind the
schemes out, by killing Hoder and letting you
think you were returned to my camp in secret.
It was known you were there. I had hopes that
the plotters would take you and turn you over
to the armies of the half beasts, in return for
the rewards their overlord had offered for runtlings. They would have had what they wanted,
and I would be rid of the danger to my kingdom."

"No dwarf, then no fall of Brosingamene, as
the signs had foretold," said Broco gently.

"Exactly. I did not tell Alane all I had
planned. She did not know the whole truth.
And she was trying in her own way to hurry
you on beyond our boundaries, by helping you
in your escape."

"Well, if I isn't just a hornswargled lump of a
stoat," began Ned, but Broco cut him short.

"Someone is looking for us, it seems. Who, I

suspect, is Doraki. And he knows what I carry, by the sound of it. That brute who followed us into the woods or some of his cronies must have means to contact their overlord. Or worse, Doraki is somewhere near here."

"What does that mean?" asked Ned, his face drawn.

"It means, Ned, that we have no time to lose in getting on our way. If they knew or suspected we were here, I'm sure that's why the Gorgolacs attacked the settlement."

"Our friend Jokim. He was very ambitious, and tried to treat with the half beasts. He wanted an army of his own, and the power that went with it. But they played him for a fool, and learned where the settlement lay. And then they knew where the prize was that they sought."

A wracking convulsion shook Garius, and he began to gasp loudly for breath.

"But I must be put in the vault, sir. I am an honorable man. I did but what I could for my people. You cannot fault me there, in fairness."

Garius jerked violently, then went rigid.

"He's done," said Cranny, removing his arm from where he had been supporting Garius' head.

"Well, I has seen and heard tell of it all now, I has. But what was he saying about a blue stone?" asked Ned, covering Garius with his cloak.

"It's the marker of Alane's door. It must be there, where he was digging."

Hurriedly the companions scouted the dark

Ruins, and soon Cranfallow called out excitedly. "Here's one as blue as a sea dabber. It's
one what I seen when we was here afore."

"Good fellow, Cranny. Now let's see to the
entry. We shall have little time, according to
Garius, before those louts find we aren't in the
settlement. We must find our way out, and
soon," said Broco, hastily picking his way to
where Cranfallow stood.

"Ain't no door, though. Leastways not one a
man could use. All rock."

"There's bound to be a way. All we have to
do is find it. Here, Ned, see what you find
there."

"Is we going to bury him up like we says we
was?" asked Cranny, "after what he was saying
he has been after, trying to turn us over, and
all?"

"Yes, we will, Cranny, if we have time."

"Well, it's all the same to me. I knowed I was
right in that feeling I had afore them Lacs
came. I knowed I felt all fluttery inside whiles
he was jawing with us."

Dwarf looked at the still form beneath the
cloak.

"He was a strange one, right enough. And
afraid."

"He ain't the only one what's ascared. I can
hear them Lacs smacking and slurping from
here."

"Then let's get on with it, quickly," urged
Broco, a cold finger of fear hammering deep
within him. He turned his mind to his digging

to keep from thinking of what could happen now that Doraki was in pursuit of him.

Dwarf set Ned to work on the right of the stone, and Cranfallow on the left. He began digging frantically about in the center, beneath the blue marker that led the way to Alane's rooms, and safety for the moment, and perhaps food and arms.

Suddenly the Arkenchest rode heavily above Dwarf's heart, a burden that was almost too much to bear.

And the Darkness now knew that he carried it.

AN ANCIENT DELVING

▧ Broco had not had time to cry out. The earth he was digging in suddenly went soft, and with a silent whooshing sound, he found himself falling, tumbling dizzily end over end, with rocks and dirt rattling in the air all about him.

He struck a steep incline painfully with his knee, then found himself in a sitting position, rocketing downward, with the seat of his pants acting as a sled. The darkness seemed to grow more dense, and he began to have trouble breathing. As quickly as it had begun, the wild plummet was over. He sat stunned and alone, as the falling debris settled about him. Staring wildly into the endless darkness about him, he sensed, more than saw, that he was in some sort of ancient chamber, long unused.

He thought at once he had stumbled onto

Garius' burial vaults, for he had said they lay below the old Ruins.

But these seemed much older. The smell of musty years stirred under his intrusion, then fell once more into empty brooding.

Dwarf carefully wiggled his toes and moved his arms to see if anything were injured, and gingerly picked himself up, finding he was all in one piece, and unhurt, except for a few sore bruises and scratches.

He peered intently upward to see if he could make out where he had fallen through, but bluish-black space seemed to run on forever in every direction.

He placed a foot in front of him, with his hands before his face to keep from bumping his nose against anything that might be there.

But there was nothing but the vast, silent darkness.

Taking a deep breath to muster his courage, he calmed himself with a slight huff and drew forth the dragon stone of his sires, and speaking softly over it, he held it before him like a lamp.

He had been paralyzed with an icy fear at first, and an old, unwanted memory lingered over his heart, of a darkness such as this, but long ago, when he had been captured by the Dark Queen.

Slowly, as one might see pale fire below deep water, the stone winked, weakly at first, then seemed to vibrate with a golden, shimmering glow.

The gleaming fire of the dragon stone leapt

forth in a sudden dazzling cone of brilliant
flashes, chasing and devouring the gloomy
shadows of the underground vault.

Broco's heart constricted and bumped hard
in his throat. His eyes, unused to the bright
light of the stone, were blinded momentarily by
the spectacle that was revealed.

Pearl-gray walls climbed beyond his line of
vision, laced and crossed with natural stone
veins, all worked into the flowing beauty of the
smooth face of the room. Inlaid ivory and
mithra caught the eye and led it along laby-
rinthine designs and patterns that went on and
on, unbroken.

And high above, near the center of the
curved roof, golden webs of light danced across
a finely wrought design work, with the
likenesses of men and elves and strange beasts
and oddly shaped castles. In the center was a
great, golden sun.

Broco gasped.

"It's dwarf work," he sighed. "Of an ancient
fashion, or I'll eat my hat."

His excitement at his discovery drew him farther into the beauty of the room.

Furnishings of wrought silver and ivory
stood about, covered with ages of dust, and
there was a stringed instrument such as he had
never before seen, but had read of in his lore
studies. It was shaped like a lyre, but upon a
deep green stand, and twice as high as his
head.

He stepped closer, and softly touched one of
the ancient strings.

It began as a humming note, below hearing, then soon all the chamber around him took it up, a muted call that sounded something between a lute and a horn.

Broco stroked the instrument lovingly, and went on, his eyes wide in wonder, the dragon stone before him.

Suspecting that these were indeed works of his forefathers, and that they had constructed some clever method to light these halls without torches or lamps, Dwarf placed the dragon stone again into the folds of his cloak.

And instead of the darkness that should have blanketed him, the very walls themselves glowed with a bright reflection of that fire. The designs came alive in fiery colors, and the golden sun high above seemed to flood the room with a soft light.

It had become like dawn in the golden room, and Dwarf gazed about in unbroken enchantment.

Far ahead, other archways spread ivory and golden arms across the darkness, all high and vaulted, with the same friezes and inlaid walls, and beyond, there seemed to be many more stretching away as far as he could see in the dim light.

Broco had started toward the center archway, which was shaped in the form of a butterfly, when faint, faraway shouts reached his reeling mind.

"Master Broco, Master Broco," came the forlorn cries. "Where is you, sir?"

Dwarf stopped short, still gazing raptly at the far doorway.

"I'm here," he called dreamily, only half aloud.

The noise of his own voice seemed to snap the spell he had fallen into, and clearing his throat, and coughing, he called out as loudly as he could. "I'm here, below you. Be careful of the drop. You should be able to see some light, if you look closely, where I was digging. Try to slide down. It's steep, so watch your step."

Broco quickly retraced his steps to where he thought he had tumbled down, and carefully scanned the roof for a sign of his rather bumpy entry.

At first he could see nothing at all but the wondrous dwarf-wrought ceiling, with fine gold and silver inlay work that fashioned the likeness of a stream and woods, with beautiful, bright-colored flowers.

At last his eye caught a break in the line of a flowing streak of the endless tapestry, and a dark, circular hole appeared in the form of a mouth on a flying, many-colored dragon.

Looking more closely, he saw that the wall in that particular place had been wrought from living stone, and it curled inward, toward the room's center.

Studying it closer still, he discovered a dry fountain bed at the wall's base, with newly dislodged stones and earth and the imprint of his own backside where he had fallen.

"Of course," he thought aloud, "A fountain.

My kinsmen were fond of using water in their designs."

He ran his hand tenderly over the worn, smooth surface of the wall.

"It must have run from the mouth of the dragon, into a fall, and ended in the fountain."

Broco fell into silent admiration of the architecture and design of the cleverly wrought waterfall, but was jerked back to the moment by more frantic calls from his friends.

"Where is you, sir?" called Ned woefully. "We doesn't see no light nowheres. It's dark as a tomb out where we is."

Dwarf stood directly under the fountain's mouth and once more held out the dragon stone, speaking the words that brought it to life as he did so.

But the eye of the stone seemed to flash into brilliant fire as soon as he took it from his cloak, and spiraling reddish-blue flames crept over the high chambers.

"Well, by the beard of Co'in," he mused aloud.

From within the flashing depths of the stone, a deep voice sang out, sonorous and lilting.

> "In times of golden halls
>   there was built
>   a fair, deep dwelling,
>   pearl-gray and fire
>   were the dragon falls,
>   beneath the waters of Fairlake,
>   below the Mellow Wood,
>   before the Dragon Wars

brought me forth,
these silent halls
have stood.
Eo'in, sire of delving folk,
carved these pillars
by his hand,
With Co'in, and his band.
Far deeper now they lay,
in time and death
they've slept,
till these darkened halls
should welcome dwarfish kind
once more,
and see the promise kept."

Dwarf wanted to ask what promise was meant, but staggered back without speaking, and dropped the stone, which had become white-hot. With a last blazing inferno of dazzling light, the stone dimmed, flickered once, then faded into a dull, throbbing, transparent reddish-gray. In another moment it had vanished entirely, leaving only a small halo of pale sparks in its place.

With a cry of distress, Broco fell to his knees and reached for the dim outline on the smooth floor where the stone had disappeared. A blistering pain tore through his arm as he touched the pale ash, and he fell back stunned.

And just at that moment, with shouts and curses, Ned and Cranfallow tumbled noisily into the fountain, followed by a small avalanche of earth and stone.

THUMB'S HAVEN

▒ "Hush," warned Thumb, raising a paw in warning.

The small band hid in the deep shadows of the trees that ringed the ruins of the old halls of Brosingamene.

"Did you hear that?" Thumb asked, after a long pause.

Otter, having just pushed Bear rudely off the paw he was standing on, had heard nothing.

And Bear, mumbling whispered apologies for stepping on his friend in the pitch darkness, heard nothing either but the angry little chirp Otter had given.

"It sounded like voices," murmured Flewingam quietly, straining to hear something further. "And man voices, at that."

"But it's stopped," went on Thumb.

"They may have heard us."

The friends hardly dared breathe as they waited in the darkness of the unfriendly woods.

Not a sound broke the stifling silence, and the rising wisps of early morning fog had begun to make ghostly gray wraiths of ordinary shadows.

Within a few moments, it was difficult to see more than a few paces around them.

"This isn't going to help matters," whispered Thumb urgently.

"Well, it's certainly not going to help whoever it is over there, either," chirped Otter.

Thumb hesitated thoughtfully, then spoke again. "There is an old shelter near here we have used before, when we hunted near the man settlement. I think it would be safer if we went there to wait for light."

Bear poked his head upward, as if trying to rise above the gray sea that had suddenly washed over them.

"Can you find it in all this soup?" he asked, looking nervously about at the threatening figures of the trees that loomed ominously out of the silvery darkness.

"It's on this side of the old stones. All we must do is keep to our noses. I could find it in worse than this."

"Then lead on, good Thumb," rumbled Bear in a low, growling voice.

"Let me hold onto one of you, so I won't get separated," pleaded Flewingham. "I don't seem to be equipped with as fine a nose as the rest of you stout fellows."

Otter chittered and held out a paw to his

friend, and grabbed Bear's thick fur with the other.

"Now we won't lose each other," he giggled, enjoying the way Bear squirmed under his firm grasp.

"There's no need to scalp me," shot Bear angrily. "And I said I'm sorry for stepping on you. Besides, I'm not going to try to run away from you."

Otter reluctantly loosened his grip, and the friends set off at a halting pace.

Thumb stopped every few steps and put his nose to the ground, or to a tree or rock.

Swirling gray forms appeared and disappeared all about them, making them nervous and jumpy, and the dawn air, which had been warm an hour before, seemed to grow colder as the morning neared. Soon they were covered with tiny droplets of the silvery mist, and even their breathing seemed to become a part of the ghostly fog.

Nothing stirred but the gray wraith shapes in the swirling air around them, and Otter noticed that as he walked along behind Bear, he could see nothing of his friend but a small patch of a reddish-brown tail.

Flewingam, who was next to last in the single line, saw nothing at all of Otter except his two small ears, which stuck up above the silver-white sea near the ground. If he had not had firm hold of the tiny animal, he would not have known he was there at all, so well did Otter blend in with the gray shadows.

After what seemed endless hours of their

halting march, they heard a faint bark from Thumb, and his voice sounded different, as if he had gone from the open air into a cavern or a thick grove of trees.

"It's here, well enough, just as we left it," he said, as the remainder of the company drew up around him.

In the dim light they could make nothing of the haven Thumb had led them to. It seemed to be rather large, once you got into it, but the companions could not tell if it was a stand of trees that formed a close ring or if it was a cave.

Bear, standing beside Otter, rose up on his great haunches and gave a whuffling snort. His ears pricked up, and he began testing the air, moving his head first one way, then another.

"What is it, Bear?" whispered Otter, alarmed at his big friend's sudden alertness.

Bear's huge muzzle raised, then lowered, and his mouth had worked itself into a puzzled frown.

"I'm not sure. But there's something here, something I can't quite put my paw on."

"Gorgolacs?" asked Flewingam, who had been close by and heard Otter's question.

"Nothing so foul as that. More old, I should say. Something that's been here a long time. But different."

Thumb shuffled silently to Bear's side.

"This is indeed an old thing, brother. Older than man, or those beasts that attacked the settlement. We found it when we first came into these woods for shelter. It's much bigger once

you go farther inside. Fornax explored a part of
it once, but never went beyond calling distance
of here. It was so large it frightened him, although he didn't like to admit it. Said it was
just an old cave, no more, and no use to us.
Said there was no sense in wandering about in
a worthless hole."

"Whatever or whoever could have built
this?" mused Otter, sitting down now and beginning to feel sleepy.

"It wasn't man, I know," replied Thumb,
turning to answer Otter. "Those Mankind in
these woods never knew about this. It's well
hidden, although you couldn't see when we
came in the fog."

"You mean even the forest men who lived
here never knew of it?" Bear asked, finding it
hard to believe that any hideout could have escaped the keen eyes of the wood patrols of Garius.

"If they did know of it, they never came
here. It's most difficult to get to," went on
Thumb. "And I would think that unless you
knew what you were looking for, you'd go right
past it. I have never seen or heard of anything
quite to describe it."

He paused a moment, and looked away
toward where the rising sun would be in another hour.

"But soon you'll be able to see for yourself."

Bear's puzzled frown grew darker.

"There *is* something here. I can't think exactly what. The old smell is like, well like . . ."

His words trailed off without finishing his thoughts.

"Like Dwarf," chittered Otter excitedly. "Exactly like Dwarf, only very old."

Otter had poked his head farther into the gloom, and now raced around Bear's seated form.

His eyes grew huge, and his ears shot up.

"That's it, Otter. It *is* like Dwarf. Then there must be some of his kind here, or they were here sometime."

"Could it have been the dwarf band Alane told us of? That Garius captured?" asked Flewingam.

"It might have been. But this smell is too old for anything I've known of. Sort of, well, old, if you know what I mean."

"Before Garius?" quizzed Otter. "Or his father, or his father's father?"

"Much before all of them, by the smell of it. It's more like a mountain now. And I have tunneled in and around and through enough mountains to know that smell when I come on it."

"You may be right at that, Bear," said Otter, dancing back toward the looming entrance once more. "I hope it gets light soon. I shall enjoy having a look at something that old."

He stopped, and turned quickly, bumping into Bear, who had followed him. "And if there's anything of this sort around, you know Dwarf will be on to it. He's got a better nose than you or I when it comes to smelling out something of his own kind."

Bear looked down at his little friend and smiled. "You're on to something there, Otter. If Dwarf is in these woods at all, he'll sooner or later find his kin."

"We'd best get a nap while we can," suggested Thumb. "We have an hour or more until light."

Flewingam snored his assent, and the friends remembered how tired they were, and bone-weary, they lay down beside the sleeping form of their companion. Thumb insisted he wasn't tired at all, and agreed to stand watch while the others slept. They were too tired to argue long, and soon Otter and Bear had snuggled down beside Flewingam, flanked on either side by the members of Thumb's band.

And all about them the sea-gray mist rolled and turned, settling down damply upon them, and flowing on into the mouth of the ancient dwelling they had chanced upon.

Thumb, who was more tired than he wanted to admit, dozed and nodded awake at intervals, snorting and smacking his lips occasionally, as he half dreamed of a bright fire, with hot bread and fresh honey.

While farther back, deep inside the shelter he had led them to, footsteps slowly padded along smooth corridors, stirring up ages of un-disturbed dust, and as silently as wind passing over water, drew near to where the comrades lay sleeping in the growing morning stillness.

THE GUARDIANS

※ "Where is we?" cried Ned Thinvoice, his eyes wide, and full of the pearl-gray light of the chamber Dwarf had just discovered.

Cranfallow moaned once, and lowered his head. "I sees it, but I isn't asking no questions. Better left alone, I says."

"It's my own kindred that delved these halls," explained Broco excitedly. "Eo'in, first, and then all the others."

Dwarf raced to run his hand over an inlaid, glass-smooth wall.

"Just look at this. Why, the tools they must have had! And what knowledge! Imagine, all this was once solid rock and earth."

His voice trailed away as he tried to imagine how the work must have been accomplished.

Cranfallow had gotten up, and painfully dusted himself off. "Is there any more of your likes here, sir?" he asked, turning to help up Ned.

"More?" mused Dwarf dreamily, wondering what Eo'in would look like. "No, I think not, good Cranny. These halls were fashioned long before the wars of the Purge, or the Dragon Wars, as you know them perhaps. Much older, probably."

"Dragon Wars? You mean them gourd tales is all true?"

Dwarf faced his friends. "You don't intend to tell me you never heard or studied of those years?"

"Oh, we has heard, right enough. My old geezer used to spin me full of all sorts of blather about them wars. How the elves, and dwarfs, and some of Mankind all got together and had a right smart time of it, what with chasing dragons and all. And them old dragons aburning up whole towns, and wolves as big as cows coming out of somewhere, ruining crops, and gnawing people, and carrying on right fiercely."

"Ned's right," said Cranny. "We has heard, right enough. But it was all sort of fun like. We didn't never put no store by none of it." He paused, and looked shyly at Broco. "Leastways, we never thought none of it was so, till we met you."

Dwarf huffed a small bit, and straightened his cloak about him. "The Purge, as the dragons were called, came forth first in the golden dawn of time here. The High King sent them so that those here would remember that the lower realms were not where they belonged forever.

If it would have been too perfect and beautiful, not many folks would ever be tempted to leave it, and return Home. But the dragons were there, right enough. You see yourselves proof of it all around you. And even yet, our maps have references to names and places. Grimm Wastes, or the Dragon Wastes, as they are known in some places, the Dragur Wood, and on and on."

Broco stopped and caught his breath, then continued.

"In my own times, I have studied the histories and lore books of those ages. Of course, my father taught me much more of it than I would expect Mankind might have record of. And being a lore master, and keeper of learning, I'm sure I was put more in a way of seeing to it all than you might have been."

Ned's eyes had grown wider as he listened.

"Does you mean they might still be hanging about?"

"Who?" asked Dwarf shortly, having warmed to his lecture, and resenting the interruption.

"Them dragons."

"The last was slain in a great battle not far from here, a long time before you or me, Ned."

"Was they on the other side?" asked Cranny. "I mean, was they in cahoots with them Lacs and Lughs?"

"All of them are of the same line. They were all spawned by the lady Lorini's dark sister. There are many more things that move upon this world that are of her making."

"Well, that's all beyond me," sighed Ned.

"What we ought to be asking after is where is we now, and how is we going to get out? And where is our friends? And is old Ned Thinvoice ever going to have any more victuals to fill him?"

Dwarf, having forgotten their danger for the moment, fell silent. He took his hand away from the mirror-bright wall and paced a short distance toward the far corridor and high arched door. He held his hands tightly behind his back and stood a moment more, his head down and his brow troubled.

"I think," he said at last, turning to his friends, "that we have lost our chance to get to Alane's old dwelling. It's no good trying to get back there."

He paused, pointing away upward in the general direction of the dragon's mouth, high above.

"We have no ropes, and the face of the wall is too smooth for footing."

Another silence, as he let this information sink in.

"You mean we is trapped here?" blurted Ned, after a moment's stunned silence.

"I didn't say that, my friend. I'm of a delving sort myself, and I have no small knowledge about the doings of my kindred. We shall explore ahead in these halls, and I'm sure there will be other entrances. This obviously was never meant for a doorway." He pointed again to the roof.

"But what of food? And water? We doesn't has none of it."

"I know, Cranny. But perhaps we shall find something farther on."

"I doesn't like the lay of this," growled Ned, remembering all his troubles with dwarf witches.

"Nor do I, Ned, but then there's really nothing else we can do."

"Well, if that's the way of it, let's us find out what we can. We hasn't got nothing to lose by it. And I don't thinks so much about putting food in my yap if I's afooting it."

"You're right, old fellow. So let's be off and see if we can't make the best of the moment."

Dwarf arranged his cloak about him, and patted the Chest to seat it securely.

Touching that small object beneath the rough cloth gave him hope once more, and his spirits rose.

"This may prove a stroke of luck yet," he said cheerfully to his companions.

"Bad or good, we is here," said Cranfallow sourly, "and we needs to be somewheres else, by my way of thinking."

"And running our jaw ain't going to move us no way," chided Ned.

"Then off we go, and keep close behind me. I think I can find the lay of this delving soon enough. I've read about it all my life, and seen drawings of what it was like."

As he finished speaking, a small, faraway scraping noise froze the friends motionless. Again it came, like stone being dragged across stone. or the noise of an old mountain creaking in its sleep. After what seemed like hours, the

sound stopped. But the utter silence was more
foreboding than the noise had been.

"What was that?" breathed Cranny.

Dwarf, straining to hear more clearly, motioned angrily for Cranfallow to be silent. He
knelt, and placed an ear to the cold, glassy surface of the floor. He remained there so long
that his friends felt sure he must have fallen
asleep.

Ned moved an arm to reach out and touch
Broco, but the little man picked that moment
to rise. His face was puzzled, and his eyes carried a worried expression.

"It's odd, but there seems to be someone else
here. I've heard definite footsteps, or something
that sounded very like them. And something
else I can't make certain of. Heavy scrapes, but
I don't know. Perhaps rocks, or something like
a mill wheel."

Cranny had gone white. "You mean we isn't
the only ones down this snake's nest?"

"No. And it isn't a dwelling for the likes of a
snake, Cranny. These were the halls of dwarfish
kings once."

"No offense, sir," said Cranfallow lamely.
"But I isn't no sort of one what's ever gone
about much outside fresh air. I always does
think of tombs, though, when I is rattling my
brain on dirt, or what's under it."

"When you is rattling your brain, you isn't
running your jaw, leastways," snapped Ned,
getting shivers from his friend's reference to
graves.

Dwarf cautioned them into silence.

"Whoever our guests are, they're below us. I suspect these halls are on three levels, as are all dwarfish works. So we must be either on the second level, or the first. There will be a meeting chamber where the levels cross. It's there we must look, for it's there we'll be able to find our exit."

"What about them others?" whispered Ned.

Dwarf smiled faintly.

"I hardly think they'll know about all the secrets," he said. "Unless, of course, they're my kind. And if that's the case, we've no worry."

He spoke to reassure Ned and Cranny, but his own thoughts were troubled. The sounds had been of what sounded like a large party, although he couldn't tell how many, nor of what sort they were. He was sure, however, it was neither Mankind nor Gorgolac nor Worlugh he had heard. And the scraping noise still puzzled him deeply. All he could be certain of was that whatever it was, it was not a heartening sound, nor one that would bode them any good.

But he caught his breath, gave his final orders to keep close, and the three set off at a quick pace, going quietly and keeping to the dimmer part of the great, glowing chamber.

As they passed through the tall butterfly-shaped archway at the far end of the hall, he saw that the chambers ahead were much fainter, and less light showed. And far ahead, he could see the darkness began again. He lamented bitterly the loss of his father's gift to him, and felt the absence of the dragon stone heavily in his pocket.

Farther on, as he had expected and feared, their progress was slowed to a tortuous crawl, and Ned and Cranny moved clumsily, bumping and knocking against strange objects in a deathlike shroud of darkness that seemed to stifle their very breathing.

And worse than the darkness were the words that kept running over and over through Broco's head, sending fingers of icy dread through his numbed brain, and a leaden heaviness settled about his drumming heart. His father's words came back to him now, vividly, as if he were sitting before the talking fire dogs in front of his own home hearth as a young spanner, listening with eager attention as the history of Dwarfdom was recited by the kindly white-haired old dwarf who sat in the low, pleasant green chair that eased the distance of all journeys. He had just heard of the Beginning, and was on now into the waning years of the Golden Kingdom.

"And when it came to pass that the enemy had entered into being, the dwarflords of olden began to retreat from sight and dealings with the others of those realms and kingdoms abroad the mantle of Atlanton. The enemy was crafty and treacherous, and began to plant the seeds of doubt and mistrust through all the Creation. And as the later lords of Underearth came into power, the Guardians were called up, to protect the entries and highways into the kingdom's underground."

Dwarf shuddered, and clasped the Chest closer to his pounding heart.

INTO THE DEPTHS

⊠ Neither Bear, nor Otter, nor Thumb, nor
any of the others heard the stealthy approach
of the padded feet. And none of the animals,
nor Flewingam, had a chance to defend themselves against the silky, sticky net that was cast
silently over them and drawn into a tight, iron
cage.

Otter, awakened by a pain in his shoulder,
coughed and spluttered, for a gluey-feeling
something had filled his mouth. But the pain
increased, and he found he couldn't move, and
the ache came from having Bear, who had been
sleeping beside him, squashed solidly against
him.

"Bear," Otter gasped angrily, "you silly ass,
you've rolled over on me. Get off."

His temper was short, and he tried to give his
big friend a kick to wake him up. To his surprise, he found he couldn't move.

146

He tried again, using all his strength, but he was held in a steel vice of a sour-smelling, sticky stuff, which tickled his nose and made him sneeze. In the next instant, he had fainted.

None of the others had ever wakened, and now they all lay senseless, bound tightly in the woven netting that smelled slightly of decayed earth, and which had drugged them all into a deep, fathomless slumber.

Knobby hands drew up cruel knots until the bonds cut deeply into their flesh, and soon, gnarled legs strained to pull the captive friends on deeper into the black hole that led on into a deeper shaft under the soft, damp-smelling floor of the woods above.

As the fog began to clear in the morning light, the mouth of Thumb's shelter slowly crept into view. Great gray slabs of immense stone ringed a yawning hole that appeared to sink into the very depths of the earth, with age-less, time-blackened trees that ringed the circular opening like gigantic teeth around the ugly mouth of a dark scar.

Had Broco been with them, or had the friends seen the place in full daylight, they would have shunned the hiding place, even at risk of being discovered by Gorgolac warriors, so foreboding was the scowling face of the cavern.

And Thumb, although he had, in truth, used the place for shelter in years past, had never been there overnight, nor had any of his band ever ventured into the foul-smelling place, although he had lied a bit about Fornax explor-

ing it, for he didn't want to frighten his new
friends with needless worry or his own misgivings about the place. It was, he knew, safe from
anything they were running from, and he did
know none of Mankind had ever found it, or if
they had, had ever used it.

It would be safe enough, he assured himself,
to lay up for a few hours, until dawn.

Yet somehow, he thought, as if in an angry
dream, he felt harsh, evil-smelling ropes about
him, and struggled vainly to escape. His mind
reeled, then for a brief moment he knew it was
no dream, but a wave of darkness washed over
him, and he knew no more.

And on and on, down and down, the comrades were dragged, farther and deeper into
the chilling night of the endless darkness under
earth, rolled and pulled and pushed, until after
a time the descent ceased, and they lay heaped
in a senseless tangle on a cold, smooth floor
that glimmered dully by the light of flickering
red eyes.

A grating rumble stirred Flewingam from the
tortured nightmare he had fallen into, and in
the half-light of the fiery eyes of his captors, he
saw, or sensed, that a wall had moved, shutting
them into an immense chamber. And the eyes
were gone, too, beyond the shifting stone that
had sealed them tightly into the solid rock of
the earth. He screamed out a warning, but
fainted with the effort, and the cold, frozen
echo of his voice went on unbroken, until at
last it died away, and nothing stirred, and the
vast, empty mountain of stone about them

seemed to tremble, as if it were a live thing, and with a long, snoring sigh, settled into an even darker silence, beyond all remembrance of sound or light.

RESOLUTIONS IN
THE DARK

"Owwwwwww," wailed Ned, for the fifth time in as many steps.

"What is it, Ned?" shot Dwarf, half angrily, because of the dreadful darkness and being unable to see anything beyond his own nose.

"I has barked my poor shin something fierce awful," moaned Ned. "And I can't sees no use to this. We isn't getting nowheres but loster. Let's us get back, and try that hole in the roof. They has to be some way we can gets out asides banging ourselfs to death in this snake's den."

"It is *not* a snake's den, my man," said Dwarf testily, although he could think of no good reason, other than his breeding, for defending it. At the moment, that was his own opinion, and he lamented the loss of the dragon stone anew.

Cranfallow blindly groped his way to where

Broco stood, and after feeling his hat to make sure it was Dwarf, and not some covered fixture he spoke to, he said, "Ned ain't one to get spooked by no gourd fancies, sir, and neither is I, for all that. But we isn't no tunnel rats, and we doesn't see so well as you. I know you has them dwarf spells and all, but I thinks we is somewheres we ought to never have been noways. And I is with Ned. I figure our only chance is to high-foot it back to where we was, and sees if we can't find no ways out there."

Cranfallow finished, and tried to see Dwarf's face. He peered closely, and bent nearer the little man, but could only make out the barest outline of Broco's face beneath the brim of his hat.

And Dwarf, beginning an angry huff at this mutinous talk, had flushed, and his features had taken on an ugly appearance that his companions could not see.

"And what is wrong with this place, I might ask? Far better than the likes of you are ever likely to crawl into again. These halls were delved by the lords of olden, kings of all Underearth."

His voice rose, until he ended in an almost shrill shout.

Ned put out a trembling hand to quiet his friend. "Don't take no offense, sir," he began, but Dwarf had brushed him stiffly away.

"And who are you to touch the descendant of Co'in?" he asked coldly. "And if you dislike it so much, you can return as you will."

"We isn't going without you, nohow," broke

in Cranfallow. "We has tagged along with you since Seven Hills, and afore that, and we isn't no Jack-come-latelys, and we isn't no Lac or Lugh that we leaves a fellow flat at the first signs of trouble. If you is for going on and trying to gets us through here, then we is with you. Even if you isn't sure, we doesn't care, we is still with you." He paused for breath, for he, too, had raised his voice. "And you is powerful mean to talks that way to your friends," he ended, an indignant tightness in his throat.

Broco's hand clutched the Chest tightly, and the words of a spell hung at the tip of his tongue. His rage flared for a moment, then something seemed to flow through him, cool and wonderful, and a sweet-smelling wind washed about his forehead. Without realizing it, he had gripped the Chest so tightly that its life had ebbed gently into the beating of his heart, and the powerful, singing strength of it flowed into him in surging motions.

For a moment he thought he saw the tower of the swan in Cypher, and the cool, morning breeze brought with it the promise of the east garden, in full bloom, and the brilliant blue and purple flowers there danced before his eyes in an unbroken field of rainbow colors, and almost like the wind, but softer, spoke the soothing, healing voice of Lorini. He could not make out the words, but he knew it was her voice, and just the tone of it was enough to lift his spirits and hopes.

And tinkling laughter, falling on his ears in soft murmurs, reminded him of the beautiful fountains that splayed their colored waters in time with the singing of the elves, as they played the sun-colored flutes and stroked the dark brown tones of their harps.

And there was the painfully beautiful face of Cybelle, gently hovering near him.

A little cry escaped him, and his small shoulders hunched and fell, as if he had been struck a sharp blow. Low, choking sobs wracked his body in waves, and at last the tears fell freely, and the black despair that had begun settling over him since entering the terrible woods slowly began to be washed away.

Ned clapped him on the back, and tried to speak, but found he was crying himself. "We isn't no good for the likes of you, I knows, sir," he blurted. "And we doesn't have no claim to your friendship. We is poor blighters that doesn't belong nowheres but on a battle line."

"Oh, Ned, you ass," bellowed Dwarf, clumsily hugging the startled Thinvoice. "I've fallen under the spell, don't you see? A dwarf is first of all a dwarf, and blast it all, we can be morose and cranky when we're underground. And seeing these halls that my sires before me built just rattled me for a moment. I can't say how sorry I am."

"There ain't no need to says you is sorry, sir. We knows you has a powerful lot on your mind, what with us lost and all. We is the ones what should be ashamed of ourselfs, snapping and jawing about going back and all, when we knows it ain't no good, and that we couldn't gets out no way."

"Hear, hear," mumbled Cranfallow, leaning close to his friends in an effort to see whom he was addressing.

The three fell silent, and in the pitch black fumbled about until they all managed to shake hands and give one another reassuring claps on the back.

Broco felt the almost unbearable pull of the atomsphere of the dwarf halls with all the fiber of his being. Page after page of books he had read filled him with the glory and honor of his sires and their fierce loyalty to each other. Time and again, in the dwarf lore he so dearly loved, were histories of deceit and betrayal in dealings with men, or elves, or animal kingdoms, and there was inbred in all his kindred the ferocious mistrust of all who were not of dwarfish lines.

He thought of his long friendship with Otter and Bear, and Greyfax, and Froghorn, and his two faithful companions who were sharing this new danger with him.

Had he been brought up in the regular drawfish manner and lived more among his own kind, these halls, and the attraction they held, would very likely have overpowered him and brought him under their spell. But he had been of a gypsy lot, not much in the company of others, and more often than not, alone, and he had been about more among other kinds than his own, and had found trust and friendship far beyond his expectations. And thinking this, he remembered Otter and Bear, and Flewingam, and their own danger.

And their errand, to get the Chest across Calix Stay, beyond the reach of the Dark Queen. The small object beneath his cloak grew suddenly so heavy he almost buckled under the crushing weight. He knew, for some reason beyond him, he was meant to play out this part of bearing the dreadful weight of the hopes of Atlanton Earth, and that there was nothing for it but to carry on.

Thoughts of Greyfax crept into his mind, and he wondered what could be keeping the wizards away so long, when their wards' danger was so great, and the Chest in the hands of so small an army as two animals and a dwarf and their friends. Surely Greyfax, or Melodias, or Froghorn would realize the great peril they were in, and set out to rescue them. Or, at least, to come for the Chest.

Dwarf shook himself out of these thoughts, and smiled to himself ruefully, knowing that the Circle knew the risks it ran, and the danger, and that he was on his own for the moment, and must carry on as best he could. He had turned to speak to Ned and Cranny, to try as he could to cheer them up, when from a lower hall, somewhere more or less off to their right, they heard the odd scraping again, as if the earth were shifting, or clearing its throat.

"It's them noises again," whispered Ned, his face more visible now in its stark whiteness.

"We has been hearing them rumbles ever since we has been standing here," confirmed Cranny, "and I doesn't know what they is, but it don't sound like nothing friendly to old Cranny or his mates."

"I think I know what they mean," began Dwarf wearily, "and you're right, Cranny, they mean no good news for us."

Dwarf broke off a moment to listen, then continued.

"Long ago, when the lords of Underearth first began delving, things were much different, and commerce between all kingdoms was free and open. All this, of course, was long before the Darkness. But then later, how much later I can't say, things began a turn for the worse, and my sires began to cut themselves off from outsiders. And matters took such a turn for the worse after the Dragon Wars that my kindred sealed off their kingdoms and returned to deeper delvings and lower realms. To protect themselves and the portals above earth, they called forth the spirits of the deepest depths of the rocks and stones that lie beyond the darkest thought of deepness. They are called the Guardians. Not anything of a nature we have ever known, for they go back to the very creation of things. And my sires had found the secret of calling them."

Dwarf caught his breath, for he had been talking very fast, trying to explain what they were up against.

"In the dwarf halls I've been in, and that's been many, this side of Calix Stay, the delvings were done much later, and the Guardians had not been called. But here, these shafts were fashioned in the First Beginning, and kept throughout the ages. And they called these things to shut off the tunnels to the outside. I think we would have been lost had we not come down the back way, so to speak, for our doorway was never one that was meant to be used as such."

"You mean them things is sort of like watchdogs?" gasped Ned, growing another shade paler.

"Exactly, Ned. And it seems the lords of these lower halls, and all their kin, have long since perished, or fled beyond the River, or elsewhere. But that would make no difference to the Guardians. They never die, to our knowledge, at least not while they are charged with their duty. So they've lasted on, and are here yet."

"That's why none of them rooms back yonder is plundered, I reckon," said Cranfallow. "There was enough jewels and such to make a man king twiced over."

"And it's also why we don't find the whole place overrun with Worlughs or Gorgolacs. They would find these halls adequate for their use. Even the Darkness cannot get past the Guardians."

"That's all well and proper, sir, and I is glad they has done eaten any loose Lacs or Lughs, but what is we going to do? They isn't no friendly sorts, by your account."

"No, Ned, they're not. They're neither friend nor enemy, really. They owe their service to the dwarflords, and carry it on as they know how best to do, and will go on doing so until they are released. I have read somewhere that they are the ghosts of evil being punished for their deeds, and that once they are freed, they return to wherever it was they came from."

"Then we isn't in no danger?" asked Cranfallow anxiously.

"Not inside," said Dwarf grimly, "for as long as we're here we needn't worry about anyone else getting in, at least. So we'll find no ugly surprises awaiting us in that quarter."

"Well, that is news that eases old Ned a good bit," whistled Ned.

"The problem lies not there, but in our getting *out*," said Dwarf.

Ned and Cranfallow gasped together.

"You mean them things won't let no one out, neither?"

"I'm afraid not. The old lords were very strict in that. They alone knew the key to gaining exit or entry. And they feared a subject might go bad, and there are bad sorts in every lot. They didn't want their whereabouts known, or any secret given away. So they placed the Guardians at their gates to keep one in, as well as out."

"Then we is here forever," moaned Ned desperately, and the words echoed grimly back from the darkness like a curse.

"There is a chance, Ned. Keep heart, old man."

"What chance is they agoing to give us?" grunted Cranny. "From all you has told us, we is as good as bones."

"If it were only you and Ned, that's true.

You'd last a day or two, and starve or die of thirst."

Ned and Cranny shuddered in the darkness.

"But there is one small difference. There is the fact that you're with a dwarf."

"Then we gets to die full of gourd tales and such, but we still ain't no better for it," replied Ned bitterly.

"Perhaps not," muttered Dwarf. "Still, they may recognize a lord of Underearth. Your luck with your dwarf witch may be turning, Ned."

Ned looked hard at his small friend, and thought he had heard something that sounded very much like a small laugh. And that, he thought, was probably the worst sign of all.

AN UNWANTED NAP

※ Far below where Dwarf stood, an iron-hard chill settled over the prison chamber where Otter lay. His breath came in short gasps, and his groggy mind was numbed with the darkness and the evil-smelling ropes that bound him. He could not tell whether his eyes were open or shut, so vast was the gloom, and any attempt to sit up or stir himself was painful, so he lay half conscious, barely breathing, listening to the only sound of life there was, which was the gasping snores of his friends next to him.

Flewingam groaned, and called out in his unnatural sleep.

Otter gathered all his strength and called out in a choking voice, his throat so dry and parched it hardly carried at all. "Bear, can you hear me?"

A muffled growl and the noise of Bear snorting were his only answer.

"Bear, old fellow," squeaked Otter again, "wake up."

The big animal coughed, and said in a stuttering, pale voice, "Otter?"

"Here, I'm here," chittered Otter weakly. "What's happened?"

"I don't know. I'm covered up with some sort of nasty slime."

"So am I. Can you get free?"

Bear yawned in reply. "I might could, if I weren't so sleepy. I keep thinking about a nap."

"Don't!" cried Otter sharply. "We're in great danger here. I don't know what's happened, but we're tied up, and in some place that sounds like a cave."

Bear's ears picked up at the mention of a cave. His jumbled thoughts immediately went to his old home, and the new honey he had stored there.

"I could use a drop or two, and a slice, now that I think of it," he said dreamily, and he began the motion of rising.

The cruel bonds dug deeper into his fur, and he fell back with a short, growling cry.

"How can I get up if you're lying on top of me?" he blurted out angrily. "And it feels as if Flewingam is there, too."

"Oh, Bear, you ass, don't you see what's happened? We've been captured somehow while we were asleep. They've tied us up."

Bear was silent a moment, taking in this information, and trying to get his reeling thoughts in order. "Where are we?" he asked at last.

"I don't know. All I remember is lying down to sleep an hour or two, until sunrise. We were in that shelter of Thumb's."

"Is Thumb here? And Flewingam? And the rest?"

"I think so. It feels like it, anyhow."

Bear heaved himself heavily onto his side, grunting painfully, and out of breath from the effort. "What are these ropes?" he snorted, thrashing this way and that, finding himself more entangled than before.

Bear's struggle ended abruptly.

"It's no good," said Bear hopelessly. "They just get tighter if you try to move."

"We have to do something. We can't just lie here like this," panted Otter, who was using all the craft and skill he could muster to slip free of the choking ropes.

He twisted and squirmed and wiggled, but the pressure of the cold cords cut deeper into his neck and hind legs, until he was almost choked. He was on the point of panic at the sensation of being unable to breathe, and was about to flail out wildly, but he found that if he was still, the strangling pressure let up. He lay back, gasping.

"It's no good," he said, when he had caught his breath. "I can't budge these nasty things."

"Can you get near enough for me to chew at them? Maybe we could gnaw them loose?"

Bear's stomach turned violently at the thought of having the evil-smelling things in his mouth, but he was beginning to be badly frightened by the cold darkness and the eerie silence.

He was not afraid of caves or bear digs, or any other kind of underground work, having been in or around them all his life. Yet this place was so dark and silent it was more a tomb than any sort of proper cave, and he wanted to be anywhere else, so long as it was away from here. It was much more silent and ominous than the underground waterway to the old rose fountain upon Havamal, and Bear shuddered, remembering their narrow escape there. But it all seemed far away, and so distant now that Bear had trouble remembering little details. And it was hard to concentrate in the stifling closeness of the pitch-black silence.

"I think maybe I can just reach this cord around my neck," chirped Otter. "But pheeeeewwww, what a smell."

"We have to try it," said Bear desperately.

"At least it'll take your mind off being hungry. I don't think I'll want to put anything in my mouth again for a while."

At the mention of food, Bear's heart fell, and he remembered the pleasant moments in his dream when he had been thinking of the kegs of new honey in his old digs.

"Perhaps it might do well enough for you, my friend, but I'm afraid I shall be too weak with hunger to chew anything, unless we start soon."

Otter didn't reply, and Bear heard the steady crunching of the little animal's strong teeth.

He lowered his head and found he could just

get his muzzle under the choking thing that ran from his paws around his back. Shutting his eyes tightly, and trying to ignore the foul smell, he carefully bit with all his strength into the thick coiled knot. It tasted like soured bark, and was as tough as stone, and he had to keep holding his breath as he chewed. His eyes began watering, and his nose ran, and a large portion of his last meager meal hung dangerously near his throat, but he bit harder and ground at the terrible, slippery thing with all his might.

A sudden explosion of chirps beside him startled him badly, and without thinking, he almost swallowed a piece of the half-chewed cord.

Gagging and spitting, he blurted out, "Now you've almost been the death of me, Otter. Do hush up. I've almost poisoned myself."

"I can move, Bear," chittered Otter, breaking into a low series of whistles. "And I've got a paw free."

Before Bear could reply, there came a rustling noise, and the sound of the words for the man spell, and a sudden tightness of his own bonds as the ropes drew taut across his chest. The pressure suddenly vanished, and he found his own forepaws were free.

"That's done it," called Otter in his man form voice. "I wondered what this clumsy shape might be good for. I've broken all but the ropes around my feet."

The big animal felt the strange hands groping for him, and soon the ropes were loosened enough for him to wiggle free from the tangled coils.

"Is Flewingam's knife still there?" asked Otter hurriedly.

Bear sat up and shook off the smelly cords. "I'll see. I can't tell what's what in this blasted hole. Can't see a thing."

He fumbled blindly and finally located the still face of Flewingam, and after a great deal of patting and pawing, finally felt the cold hilt of the dagger.

"It's here."

"Good. See if you can cut the others free. I'm going to see if I can find out where we are, or what sort of place this is."

Otter stood.

"Owww," he cried, banging his head painfully.

"Low roof, it seems," muttered Bear.

"Too low for this gangly body, anyhow," replied Otter, once more repeating the words, and feeling his own familiar shape return. He wiggled his tail comfortably and set out anew.

Bear had almost finished the impossible task of trying to cut his companions free, having to feel carefully to make sure he would hurt no one in his blind slashing, when Otter called out, his voice faint and far away.

"I think there's water of some sort, Bear. It's wet, but I don't like the smell of it. It doesn't seem to be moving."

There was a muted splash, and a rippling sound.

"Ugh. Dead water, by the feel of it," said Otter. "And a lot of it, by the sound."

"Anything else?" called Bear.

"Stone walls all the way to here. Low roof. No light anywhere."

"No doorway, or any holes?"

"Not that I've found. At least not yet," Otter forced himself to say, for in his mind he was beginning to feel that being free of the ropes was no matter, for there seemed to be no way out of the solid rock walls that had swallowed them. And the water he had found, which would have been the best discovery of all, had an oily texture to it, and smelled as water did when it had stood long in a deep well. Dead water, as he had told Bear.

And in the pitch blackness, he thought of all the unpleasant things that could still live in such a black pool, and he quickly backed away from the slippery brink.

The water was on the same level as the cold, smooth floor, and one started where the other ended.

"How deep is it?" asked Bear, now moving cautiously toward him.

"I don't know. I hate to touch it."

"Do you think maybe it's just a flooded passage? It may be just standing in the tunnel, and not a regular sort of river or pool at all. Or pond, or whatever."

Otter considered that a moment.

"You might be right, Bear. The walls are low, and run right into it. And there's no proper bank, or landing, or anything like that."

"Then perhaps we should try wading in a bit, and see if it goes on somewhere."

"It seems to be the only way not blocked," agreed the little animal. "But I don't fancy a swim in that."

He felt Bear's huge form brush by him, and heard the shivering woof of his friend.

"It's cold enough," he said.

"Be careful there. It's slippery as ice."

A large splash and flailing of water followed his warning, which had come too late.

Otter was drenched by the wall of water that had engulfed him, and he spluttered and gasped in the frozen wetness.

"Bear," he wailed, "are you all right? Wheeeewup, this is freezing."

"I-I-I-I-I'm f-f-f-ine," stuttered his friend, his big teeth chattering loudly. "I can stand up."

With a swooshing sloop, Bear floundered back to the dry stone floor and shook himself vigorously.

"That's one way to get the spider's nests out of your head," he stammered.

"And a good way to get a quick nip, too," spluttered Otter angrily.

"At least we know it's not deep," replied Bear indignantly, shaking himself again.

"What's happened there?" came the weak voice of Flewingam.

"Oh, Flew, so you've finished your nap, have you? Well, we've already been up, had break-fast, and a bit of a swim."

"Breakfast?" came the hopeful voice. "But

what's happened to the light? I thought it was almost morning hours ago."

"It is," shot Otter, "anywhere but in this worm's nest."

"A hole? I thought it sounded like an echo."

"Hole, indeed," muttered Bear. "It's a shaft I doubt even a worm would take kindly to."

A low, whuffing grumble told them Thumb had roused himself, followed by other snorts, snuffles, coughs, and grunts.

"Hullo, what's all this?" squealed Lilly, then fell into a fit of sneezing.

"Don't try standing, Flew. You'll get a nasty bump."

"Where are we?" asked Thumb.

"Now, Lilly, don't cry," warned Bear.

Several other voices spoke at once, and the cavern echoed noisily. Otter was trampled by two of Thumb's party, and despite Bear's warning, Flewingam bumped his head sharply on the low roof of the shaft's ceiling.

"I'm blinded, I'm blinded," shouted Storm and Elam together, and a great commotion broke out somewhere to Otter's front.

"Oh, stop it, you two," scolded Thumb in a grave tone. A solid cuff sounded over the noise the two younger bears were making.

Bram, Ham, Lilly, Cress, and Cryis had begun to moan and rattle low in their throats.

"Stop it this minute," roared Thumb. "How can we make plans with you all making such an uproar? I can't hear myself think."

"Well said," agreed Bear. "And if you'll all

stop where you are, we'll count noses. It's so
dark here, I'm not sure I'm even here myself."

"Hear, hear," growled Thumb. "It's a start."

"Thumb, are all yours here?"

"Can't you hear them for yourself?"

"Good. And then Otter, and Flew. And myself, of course." Bear paused, and pinched himself to make sure. "Now to council."

"There doesn't seem to be much council to
hold," said Otter glumly. "There are only the
walls, or the water. And we can't march
through solid stone, as much as it would help if
we could. So it's that nasty water, or stay here
until someone finds us, or our friends who put
us here come back. Or?"

"Then there's only the water, if it is indeed
water at all," said Flewingam, who had paced
forward and dipped a hand quickly into the
oily pool. "Still, it seems to be a tunnel, and it
leads out of here. And it's not so deep that we
can't wade it."

"If what you say is true, brother, then it
seems we waste our breath talking. Let's get on
with the walking."

Thumb's voice was a little thin, and he was
hoping very much that no one would remember
it was his plan to come to the place to begin
with, now that it had turned into such a nightmare for all of them.

"All for it, then, it's the water. Here, take
hold of this foul thing," said Bear, holding out
an end of one of the slimy ropes that had
bound them.

Otter, thinking of the foul pool, had once

more changed into his human form, so he could
wade easier and stand higher. Remembering to
duck his man form head, he took the slippery
cord and passed it on back to Flewingam.

"Now, Thumb, give it to your bunch. Make
sure no one loses hold. We don't know what's
ahead, or where it may take us, and we don't
want to be losing anyone, if we can help it."

Bear had held his breath and slipped into
the chilling pool, and now stood, the oily water
coming up to his knees.

"Off we go. Keep hold of the rope. And try to
go as quietly as we can."

Explosions of breath and small shrieks and
gasps filled the low cavern as the companions
one by one entered the dark, freezing surface
of the oily water.

"It-it-it-it-it's so c-c-c-old," chattered Lilly,
who was next in line behind Flewingam.

"Refreshing," rumbled Bear, gritting his
teeth and pretending to himself it was exactly
like the high mountain streams he had often
swum in on the peaks of his old home across
Calix Stay. And thinking that, he remembered
it was there again they were making for, to protect the Chest.

Then the memory of the day before came
tumbling back, and he thought of Dwarf, lost,
perhaps even taken by the Darkness, and his
hopes fell.

And he noticed with some alarm that the
water in the shaft had risen from below his
knees almost to his chest.

"And not much prospect for breakfast, either," he said half aloud, grimly forcing himself onward, and resolutely putting all thoughts out of his head, except to see the pure golden rays of sunlight again, and to feel the soft kiss of a breeze upon his troubled brow.

There were many whispered cries of disgust and distress as the water rose almost to their chins, but the company pressed onward in the chilling darkness, until the smallest of the bears, which was Lilly, was forced to put her forepaws on Flewingam's shoulders to keep from going under the inky-black surface.

In one sickening moment it occurred to Bear that the shaft was leading slightly downward as they went on and that soon the water would fill the shaft completely.

It was also then that he heard the dark voices.

BELOW SUN AND SKY

THE DARK VOICES
BEGIN

※"Time and dust
    and rusty earth,
        from silent waters
           comes our ancient birth,
    below the sun,
        below the sky.
        We are the Roots,
           we never die."

Bawoooooom, Bawoooooom.
And like huge hands clapping, the shaft trembled with the noise of stone against stone.
Bits of the roof above gave way, and soon a soot of solid rock ground to fine powder began sifting onto the companions.

"Mortals frail
    of flesh and bone,
        what task have you

in our sacred home?
      We are the Roots,
        we never die."

Bawooooom, Bawooooom.

Bear stumbled backward, and crushed Otter against the shaft wall.

"Back, back," shouted Bear, wallowing to his feet again.

Mass confusion and terror overtook the smaller animals, and they began splashing and bellowing back the way they had come, wailing in quaking voices, and dropping the line they had been holding onto.

Flewingam felt the cord torn from his hand, and at the same instant Bear's great hulk bore down on him, and he was afraid of being drowned in the runaway onslaught.

Then Bear was past, and he rose spewing and spluttering, helped to his feet by Otter, who had suffered the same treatment, and who now called out in his grandest manner, hoping his voice wasn't too trembly to carry.

"Animal kings from over the River,
    friends of the lady and lords of Cypher,
      Olther, descendant of Othlinden,
          and Bruinlen, of the line of Bruinthor,
          bid you their service,
              and travel in peace."

Bawooooom, bawooooom, came the stones shuddering again, and the deep, hollow voices boomed forth once more.

"Well spoken, lords of the sunlight
        from across the Great River.
                Animal kings are welcomed here.
    Long has it been
        since our journeys brought us
            together again,
                for we are the Roots,
                we never die."

Bawooooom, bawooooom.
"Do Your Excellencies have light?" chirped
Otter, "that we may see you?"
    Bawooooom, bawooooom.

"There is plenty of light,
        oh noble stranger.
    We can see you plainly.
        The Roots have their light
        in darkness only,
        and see without eyes,
                and hear without ears,
    We are the Roots,
            we never die."

    "Can you help us out of here, sirs? If you
have no light, would you kindly show us your
doors, so that we may trouble you no longer?"
    Bawooooom. Bawooooom.

"There are no doors for Roots,
        nor windows to the sky,
                for we are the Roots,
                and never die."

"Pardon me, sirs," put in Flewingam, "then is there any way you know of that leads upward?"

Bawooooom. Bawooooom.

"Only downward, to our homes,
        do these paths and roadways go,
                but dwarfish lords dwelled here
                long ago,
                and have many shafts
                        that lead from below."

"At least we didn't get the 'We are the Roots, we never die' again," mumbled Otter under his breath to Flewingam.

But his ears had perked up at the mention of dwarfs.

"If I might," broke in Bear, who had regained his composure somewhat, and called out from some distance behind them, "could I ask the most gracious gentlemen where we are?"

Bawooooom. Bawooooom, clacked the stony notes.

"You are with the Roots," came the simple reply.

"You said something about dwarflords and halls. Are we in something like that now?" asked Flewingam, beginning to believe that even though the strange, hollow voices did not seem to be hostile, they certainly did not seem to be overly wise.

Bawooooom. Bawooooom.

"Roots came first, then dwarfish halls,

> they tore our hair, and broke our ribs,
>   and made us into dwarf-wrought walls."

Bawooooom. Bawooooom.

Thoroughly confused, Otter asked in a faintly peevish tone, "I'm sure that must have been very unpleasant for you, and I hope you feel better now. But we are lost, and don't feel so chipper ourselves, and it would be a great deal of help to us if you could give us a little more information than that. You see, we're not so old, or able to live down here as you, and we need to find our way out."

Bear cleared his throat. "Ahem. Yes, you see, it's different for our sort, being down here. And I'm a bear, and used to going about in a shallow cave, to eat and sleep in, but this," and here he gestured to indicate his surroundings, although no one could see, "this is something entirely different."

Bawooooom. Bawooooom.

"Out? Where is Out?" boomed the dark voices.

"Out," explained Flewingam, "is somewhere upward, above where we are now."

Bawooooom. Bawooooom.

"You mean the Endings?" came the booming voices, almost in disbelief.

> "Years have sealed our hearts within,
>   and no living Root has seen the Endings,
>   far above, where air grows thin,
>   and the earth is rended."

"That's it, the Endings, as you call it," chirrupped Otter. "Only it is the door back to where we belong, you see."

Bawooooom. Bawooooom.

> "It is said in stories old
> that living things do dwell beyond,
> but we have never seen them."

"If you had a torch about you, you'd get a look now, well enough," snapped Bear, his fear replaced by the irritability he felt at the monotonous, hollow black voices.

Almost imperceptibly at first, but growing stronger, a dim gray glow had spread about them.

It wasn't light, as such, but rather an absence of darkness, an eerie glimmering of phosphorescent shadow that appeared within the depths of the stone walls and roof.

"What's that?" squealed Lilly, and in her fright, she pushed Flewingam under the oily water, thrashing and sputtering.

Directly before Otter, something had moved, or shifted, like a shadow slipping from dark to light, or a gray flicker of motion that was almost unseen.

Bawooooom. Bawooooom.

> "And so we see now,
> our eyes unfold,
> to look upon
> these kings of old."

Where the voices had come from the utter
darkness before, the companions now saw, or
rather got the impression, that they came from
the walls themselves.

Nearer, a gray, shapeless mass of stone took
on a rough appearance of a huge face, its nose
chiseled and square, and where the eyes would
have been, a soft halo of silvery gray luminescence
flickered dimly.

As Otter looked closer, and his own eyes adjusted
to the poor light, he saw that the entire
shaft in front of them was alive with the same
vague outlines.

"Well, that's better. Thank you kindly, good
Roots," blustered Bear, squinting, and looking
about in relief.

Bawooooom. Bawooooom.

"It is the first time in many ages we have
opened our dark eyes, for travelers seldom
wake us."

"I shouldn't imagine so," agreed Flewingam.
"Not that it isn't a lovely place, and all."

"Oh, please," begged Lilly, "can you show us
how to get back to where we were?"

Flewingam braced himself at once, but the
small animal made no move to dunk him again.

Bawooooom. Bawooooom.

"There are no doors out, but many doors
in,
    to the bottom of time, and back again,

except down beyond the Under Tide,
a cavern exists that has its tail outside."

"That's right," shouted Otter. "Or at least I
think you said something to the effect that
there is some way out of here, after all."

His eyes were growing used to the watery
gray light now, and he had begun to see the
lips, or what would have been a mouth, move
as the Roots spoke.

The whole wall shuddered, and the booming
voices seemed to escape from the very core of
the earth.

"Oh, isn't it wonderful," crooned Lilly, clapping her forepaws together in excitement. "We
shall get to leave here, and soon."

Bear asserted himself once more, rather
shamefully, from where he stood beside
Thumb.

"That's all well and good, but just where is
this cave tail that goes out? And what's the Under Tide? And is there any manner of food we
can eat or water to drink down here?"

Bear tried to be extremely casual in his questions, but at the mention of food, his voice became tight again.

He was sure his scare earlier had been because of an empty stomach.

Bawooooom. Bawooooom.

"There is food aplenty all around,
pleasant water, rich black ground.
And the Under Tide is many miles
beyond the Stairs of the Second Levels."

"Miles? Second Levels?" gasped Bear. "None of us would last to see it," he groaned.

"Cheer up, old fellow," chirped Otter. "We're not done yet. At least we know there is a way out."

"Fancy lot of good that will do us," Bear snapped. "We'll all have starved long before we get close enough to think about it."

"I think not, Bear," Otter said, then addressed the strange beings again. "Could you tell us how to reach this cave you speak of, sirs?"

Bawooooom. Bawooooom.

A deep rumbling stirred the shaft, and the gray walls seemed to ripple. Stone dust sifted slowly over the companions, and the smooth floor at their feet seemed to dance beneath them. The Roots appeared to be talking among themselves, and the words were jumbled and slurred, and hard to make out, although Otter did distinctly hear something that sounded like "too sleepy," and "much too long a trip."

After more grinding noises, the watery light blinking on and off several times, the decision seemed to have been reached, and a single dark voice spoke.

"I am Kore, the Root, and I shall guide you to Under Tide, and beyond."

"Thank you, Kore," replied Otter, "That is most kind of you."

"Won't your friends be going, too?" asked Flewingam.

"We Roots are slow and thoughtful things,

not hasty in our ways. The others stay to see
what tomorrow brings."

"Tomorrow," grumbled Bear, "is most likely
to see the end of all of us from hunger. Or dead
of thirst."

Bawooooom. Bawooooom.

> "This water at our feet is pure and fine,
> and full of rest and dreams."

"Ugh. That may be true for Roots, but it
feels brackish to me," said Thumb.

Bear agreed heartily.

Flewingam cupped his hand and brought a
few drops to his lips. He screwed up his face,
closed his eyes, and swallowed.

Otter saw the move, and cried out too late to
warn his friend. A strange look of bewilderment
crept over Flewingam's face, and his eyes
opened wide. He gave a little gasp, and swallowed again.

"Is it poisoned?" asked Otter, his voice rising
in a helpless tone.

"It's good," managed Flewingam, and bent
to drink from the dark water again.

"And it feels good," broke in Lilly, who had
been dying to drink since they first found the
water, but was afraid to until she had seen the
human taste it.

Bawooooom. Bawooooom.

> "It is food of the Roots, this magic dew,
> made by time and mountain's brew."

All the companions now splashed and sprayed each other with the stuff they had waded into, and each took long, gulping swallows of it, having to hold their eyes shut at first, and trying not to smell the brackish odor that filled the nose with unpleasant thoughts.

After a few mouthfuls of the refreshing drink, Bear turned to Lilly. "I wasn't really afraid back there a minute ago, you know. Concerned for you youngsters, that's all. Didn't know what sort of mess we'd landed ourselves in, and wanted to make sure you all got to safety."

He looked about him at the others, trying to see what sort of reply they would make to his excuse for bolting, but they were all too busy gulping the wonderful Root food to pay any attention to anything he was saying.

"Is this something like a food stream for you Roots?" asked Otter, remembering his manners at last, and not wanting to offend these strange new allies.

A hollow, ringing roar came in reply, startling the friends, but after it ceased, they recognized it as laughter, deep and hollow, and rather ear-shattering in its sudden clamor.

"Our guests don't eat with their feet," boomed the voice of Kore.

Bawooooom. Bawooooom.

"They nod, how odd," echoed the others.

Otter stared about him in confusion, then saw what the Roots had found so funny. They seemed to absorb their food from the pool through what might have been called their feet.

"Well, we have mouths, you see," he explained. "And I know it would be awkward living here like this, but we really do belong outside."

Bawooooom. Bawooooom.

"Indeed, indeed, let's make all speed, so I may return and finish my feed."

"We're ready, Master Kore, sir," said Bear, who had once more taken the lead.

"And will you leave your eyes open so we may see?" chirped Otter. "We're very clumsy in your world, and not made half so nicely as you for going about in the dark."

"I shall lead you in light to the Under Tide. From there, you will need no eyes of mine to see your way." And so saying, Kore began to move.

It looked to the companions as if an avalanche of solid stone were going to fall down upon them, for the gray mass of the wall before them seemed to part and move. With another rumbling sound, what appeared to be a stone about a man's height shifted from the solid mass of the wall and with amazing speed was suddenly far down the passage in front of them.

Bawooooom. Bawooooom.

"Goodbye, outlanders, good speed, good
    speed.
    We are going to finish our feed,
    for we are Roots,
    and never die."

Bawooooom. Bawooooom.

"Goodbye, kind Roots. And thank you," chorused the companions.

They turned and hurried on as fast as they could, toward the gray light falling on the dark water far ahead.

As they passed the last of what they could make out to be the huge forms of the Roots, the watery light where they had been disappeared as suddenly as it had come, and deep, gurgling noises began as the Roots once more began their feast.

"It must seem awfully rude of us, walking in their food like this," offered Otter to Flewingam, who now waded beside him.

"I don't suppose it matters. Not many guests, I wouldn't imagine. And their table manners are a bit odd themselves."

"I'd wager we're the only guests they've ever had," muttered Bear, speaking over his shoulder, and still very embarrassed over his unseemly fright.

"Perhaps not, brother," replied Thumb from behind. "I've seen bones since the light came."

The companions shuddered, and pressed on, walking carefully.

"I just hope their soup doesn't get any deeper," grumped Bear flatly, bringing to their attention the fact that the level of the Roots' water had been rising steadily as they went on.

Soon they had caught up with Kore, who had paused a great distance ahead of them and turned to wait. As they drew even with the

thick Root, the dark water lapped about their
chins, and the smaller animals were forced to
float and be towed clumsily along behind.

Otter resisted the very great temptation to
change forms and have a swim. And Lilly was
on the point of crying again when Kore's form
rippled forward in a gray swimming motion,
and the companions were hard pressed to keep
pace with the flickering, shadowy gray form of
the Root as he disappeared into the gloom
ahead.

GLIMPSES OF ETERNITY

⊠ "Even now your dark sister's hold upon Atlanton Earth wanes, my lady," said Cephus
Starkeeper, sitting at the great window that
overlooked the patterns of stars and universes
in the Meadows of Windameir.

"How so, my lord? Does she not yet hold my
child? And is not Cypher fallen to her hordes,
even as we speak?"

Lorini's voice was older, and the musical
quality that flowed through the words was
fainter. She looked very pale, and her clear
gray-blue eyes had clouded.

"That is so, my dear daughter. It is indeed a
sad season. But the tide is beginning to turn.
The threat is by no means ended, it's plain
enough to see. And there may yet turn an ill
wind for us all, if the Chest is lost. But good
Greyfax has rallied the beings beyond time's
end, and Faragon's armies stand upon the

threshold of victory in the realms he has now entered, those realms within realms which make up the complex existence of Atlanton Earth, and all the Atlanton Earths that there are. And as you well know, even Origin and Maldan are not beyond recapture." Cephus paused, and went on in a softer tone.

"And it was not theirs to have a Cypher or a Lorini to watch over them, or at least not in the same, full capacity as Atlanton Earth. And the Five were not yet gathered to defend them."

"Is it my part to remain here, my lord?"

"For a time, my daughter, for a time, although the hour draws near when you shall return to where your heart yearns."

"I feel it but my duty, sir. I have much left undone before I seek these halls forever."

"You speak truth, my dear lady. No, it is not yet time for you to seek these halls. The work of our Lord is not yet done, and we must see it through, as he wishes."

"Is Greyfax near at hand?"

"We may look in upon him, if you wish."

"I would like that, I think."

Cephus rose and crossed the shimmering floors, whose surface held many gleaming silvery fires, as if stars shone below them through polished mirrors. He took down from the high row of books a golden bound volume so large it nearly covered the shelf it stood upon, and placed it on the long pearl-grey table.

"Here, I think," he smiled, and opened the heavy tome to about midway.

The dazzling white pages burst into brilliant

sheets of diamond flames, and a soft strain of music filled the room with whirling echoes of flutes and strings.

As Lorini bent to look upon the startling pages, a whisking gray cloud appeared, spinning with blue and green and darker bolts of crimson across the edges, and mists focused, then receded, and a flaming river of molten yellow flowed through what appeared to be tall mountains, blue at the tops, and covered with a faint trace of blazing snow and ice.

Almost at the same moment, there came into view a raging flood of armies clashing in a broad realm of purple light, and at the center of this whirlwind of action, Lorini saw the familiar form of Greyfax Grimwald, his face terrible and grim, beneath an odd-shaped helmet that was covered with a woven net laced with branches from the thick trees that seemed to grow all around them, like dark green, shimmering things.

The battle exploded angrily all about him, but he looked up, straight into the troubled eyes of Lorini, and the grave countenance gave way to a hopeful smile, and his own eyes were clear and shining.

She could almost make out his words over the mighty roar of the colliding armies.

"What is he trying to say?" shouted Lorini to Cephus, for the room was filled with exploding lights and sharp reports, and a droning rattle rolled on like a thundering, angry sea upon a rocky shore.

"He says good cheer. This is to be a decisive

battle upon the plain he is upon at the moment."

"And Froghorn?"

"Beyond the edge of that realm, and victorious."

"May I see?"

"For a moment. Yet you will have to search hard to find him."

Cephus chuckled softly to himself, as if at something Lorini had not quite caught.

He turned one more large, golden white page, and there came immediately into view a very stern-looking man, sitting at a writing table, poring over a book almost as large as the one Lorini was gazing into.

A great array of odd-shaped pens and many discarded sheets of writing paper littered the small, book-lined room, and the stern figure seated at the writing table wadded up another as she watched, and flung the ball of paper away with an exasperated snort. This scene went on for three more outbursts such as the first, and then, almost as if he were aware of her eyes upon him, the gaunt figure glowered up from his work.

There was something amazingly like amusement in his eyes, which danced with laughter, and the turned-down frown slipped into an almost surprising smile. The features were none she had ever seen before, yet she knew without asking that the bent figure of the writer was none other than her own impetuous young Fairingay.

"Whatever is he doing?" asked Lorini, puzzled by the strange vision of the book.

"Creating and causing with his pen the same things that Grimwald is doing with his sword."

"But I thought Fairingay was to gather an army to strike for the Circle?"

"And so he has," went on Cephus, turning back a few pages.

And amid another battle roaring to life across that page rode Faragon Fairingay, at the van of a host of soldiers who were tall and fair, who carried gleaming silver shields with bright golden designs upon their depthless surfaces.

A page forward, the same Fairingay appeared dressed in deep green and gray, with a short, blunt firearm.

Another page, and the young Faragon appeared as an old man, bent with years, huddling near a fire, surrounded by many glowing young faces, who all looked at him with unconcealed awe and love.

Then came more pages of Greyfax, first in one setting, then another. He, too, like Froghorn, put on many guises, and backgrounds all flowed and wove themselves into an ever changing tapestry in the startling white aura of the book.

And along with Froghorn and Greyfax came pages of Melodias, and Greymouse, known within the Circle as Mithramuse Cairngarme.

A page flickered forward, and for a brief moment Lorini saw Cybelle dressed in rags, sitting beside an older figure of Lorini herself, at the edge of a cool green pool that lay in the center of a small clearing in what appeared to be a thick growth of elders. Around them, in a rough circle, squatted men, gaunt and weary, with the haunted, wary looks of those who are hunted.

"Enough!" cried Lorini. "I cannot bear more."

"As you wish, daughter. Although there is nothing there to be disheartened of."

"What does it mean? I don't understand."

"It means, my dear lady, that we go on with our parts, whatever they are, and to whatever lot we are cast."

Cephus slowly shut the huge volume, and carefully replaced it upon its shelf.

"You see, it's all a puzzle when you see only portions of it. Yet it has a pattern to it all, whether we see or understand it at all." He turned and smiled somewhat sadly at Lorini. "It comes and goes throughout all space, all being, and goes on until we begin to see what it all has meant." A soft chuckle escaped him. "And then we begin to see what was there all along. And the pieces fit. And then it's over, for by then we have discovered what it was all heading us toward."

"And where might that be, my lord?"

"Home, my dear. Quite simply, Home."

Before Lorini could question Cephus Starkeeper further, a page entered and bowed to her, then addressed himself to the older man.

"Beg pardon, sir, but Erophin wishes to see you at once in the Council."

"Did he say upon what errand, lad?" asked Cephus, gathering his cloak about him.

"Only that it concerns a dwarf, sir."

"Then let us make haste. Much hangs now by the beard of one small fellow who carries the Chest."

"May I come, my lord?" asked Lorini.

"As you wish. But let us not tarry. I fear it must be of some importance if Erophin feels the need to call Council."

They wound their way through the spiraling, musical halls, and soon found themselves in the Hall of Council, with its tall chambers, and great windows that overlooked the starry eyes of all the Meadows of Windameir.

A silent figure at a low desk sat studying a small disk of startling white light. Its fire leapt and darted from its surface, and touched the beard and forehead of Erophin with a flashing brilliance.

Around the spacious chamber sat other members of the Council, all silent, and waiting for Erophin to speak. Lorini had seen most of the Masters of the Circle, although there were a few there she did not recognize.

At length Erophin's gaze died away from the fiery disk, and he looked tired and strained.

"Ah, it's good of you to grace us with your presence, my lady. Come in, come in. Here, sit next to me." Erophin indicated a carved chair beside him. "I think our lady is known to all of you, although I think she knows not you all."

He nodded to an aging man on his right

hand. "Caliman," he said, nodding, "the lady Lorini."

The old man nodded in return, and bowed slightly as he sat.

"A friend of your father's," explained Erophin briefly to Lorini.

"And here's Alomen."

Alomen, a stout, cheerful-looking elderly man with smiling, clear blue eyes, beamed at her and gave a short motion with his hand that she took as a wave.

"Now to business."

"You spoke of a dwarf, my lord. I assume it is that to which we apply our minds?" asked Cephus.

"Precisely. News has reached me from His Grace that is of most urgent import."

Erophin fingered the small disk before him, and a faint, lyrical hum filled the room, coming from the depths of the now faintly glowing object before him.

"My lady, you are yet to return once more to your old realms. Not, of course, to the halls of Cypher, for that would be most tragic, at the moment. But farther, beyond Calix Stay, and into the Mountains of Beginning, you are to await our small friend and his companions. They shall have sore need of you shortly."

"Is that necessary, my lord? She has only just come from there. And I feel she hasn't had time to refresh herself from the ordeal of Cypher." Cephus sounded deeply concerned, and touched her arm reassuringly as he spoke.

"I know, dear Lorini, what a seemingly hard

task is laid to your charge. But I can assure
you, it will hasten your most dearest wish into
reality."

"Cybelle?" breathed Lorini quickly.

"That first, my lady, and then the absence of
any desire at all. But it is never our lot to alter
or in any way meddle with what is given to us
in the Book, for it is all his will. However, there
are instances where we may merely hasten, or
enhance, as it were, what was going to happen
all along. It was not given that you should return to Cypher, as it was, and that you shall
not do. However, by returning to Calix Stay,
and beyond, we may better ourselves upon
many fronts, and see the Chest safely away
from the risk of its capture upon that lower
realm."

"As you wish, my lord. When shall I leave?"

"I would prefer to say after you've further
rested, and regained your strength. However,
that cannot be, if we are to achieve our hopes."
The old man's brow knitted as he spoke, and a
faint trace of a frown crossed his fair features.
"I can send you now, if you're willing."

"Of course, my lord. I am ready," said Lorini, bowing.

"Your instructions shall be made known to
you there."

"Yes, my lord."

"I trust we shall meet upon merrier terms
soon," concluded Erophin.

He had risen, and crossed to embrace Lorini
gently.

"Stout heart, my girl. It is only for us to hold

to the Light. We must remember that, above all."

Lorini was weeping softly into her hands.

"Here, here, that will never do, old girl," said Cephus thickly. "We'll have it all to do again, if we don't give it our best efforts."

"No, I'm all right, really," said Lorini, drying her eyes with the back of her hands and trying to smile. "I haven't felt the need to cry in ever so long. It's all right now. I know it's confusing, and I must stick to my errand. I'm fine now."

And to prove it, she let out a warm laugh, as of old, in the better days of Cypher.

"I simply forget the meaning of it all from time to time. I've let myself slip into feeling I'm in control of what's to happen or not to happen."

"There, there, my dear," soothed Erophin, breaking into a smile himself. "It is all a portion of what we are here to learn. Lessons, merely lessons. And to reach the top, one must needs start at the bottom."

Lorini clasped the older man's hands warmly for a moment. "I really am ready now, my lord," she said.

"I know. His Light upon us all," said Erophin, smiling into her eyes with a gentle firmness that lit up his face with a soft, glowing radiance.

The Council Hall spun giddily for a brief moment, and Lorini saw each face there in sharp focus, each turned to her in the same bright halo of light, and her heart was calmed, and she felt her strength grow once more inside

her, and the calm peace she had forgotten since
Cybelle's capture by her dark sister returned. A
fountain of sparkling, towering rainbow colors
engulfed her, and she felt the silent singing of
the Meadows of Windameir all about her, and
saw the faint glimmer of stars and worlds, and
realms beyond number glide swiftly by her, as
she made her way toward her return to the
now dimming fields beyond Calix Stay, on beyond where Bear, Dwarf, and Otter had dwelt
in their long stay in the Meadows of the Sun,
up into the wild green lands that marked the
ending of one world and the first dim seeds of a
new.

Hazy recollections of Greyfax and Froghorn
reeled before her, and she recognized, not by
sight, but by a secret knowledge, the places
they had been, and with a sudden gladdening
of her heart, she realized that her dear friends
were there where she was bound.

She opened her eyes with a start, and found
herself gazing into the amused blue-gray smile
of Greyfax Grimwald, who sat on the edge of a
low table before a merry fire, wearing a look
that said he had been expecting her arrival for
quite some space of time.

THE FOUNDATIONS

▨ Whatever he had read in all his lore books and histories of his ancient kinsmen and whatever small skills he possessed on his own did not help Broco now.

They had come to an immense chamber, larger than any they had passed through, which they discovered by the sudden ringing echo of their own voices. The air was different. It felt almost as if they had stepped outside, and although the darkness remained as black as before, the place seemed lighter.

Ned Thinvoice started to speak, but fell painfully over an object he had stumbled across.

"Be careful," warned Dwarf, the sudden noise and clatter frightening him badly.

All their nerves were by now drawn to the breaking point.

Cranfallow had shot straight up at the disturbance, but no one noticed this.

"I isn't going to have no shinbone at all, if I keeps on barking it," moaned Ned, picking himself slowly up. "Or no elbows, neither, for all that. I feels like I has been skint so many times, I can't has no skin left on me nowheres."

Ned was unaware for a moment that he was seeing Broco and Cranfallow as he spoke, for his eyes had grown so accustomed to the pitch-black gloom that the faint light that had begun growing in the chamber went unnoticed. And then he realized he was looking at his friends, and that their eyes were wide and their mouths gaping open.

"What is it?" cried Cranfallow, raising an arm to cover his face.

"Dragon stone," replied Dwarf in disbelief.

He had knelt by the object Ned had stumbled over, and was touching it gingerly. It was a large vase, or urn, of clear, polished stone, cut and fashioned in intricate design, and inside were the glowing fires of the dragon stone.

"You must have awakened it, Ned," said Dwarf over his shoulder. "Why, it's exactly like the one I lost."

Broco had run his hand into the neck of the urn, and drew out the faintly glowing object. He examined it closely by the pale light it gave off.

"It is the stone I lost," said Dwarf, his voice full of excitement and wonder.

Before Ned or Cranny could bend down to look at Dwarf's find, the darkness was suddenly swallowed by a high, brilliant blue sheet of dancing emerald fire. The tall, carven chamber leapt into dazzling relief, rising upward and away over their heads until they were all staring straight up at a sort of dome that seemed so far away it must have been the sky, although they could see after looking at it a moment that the sparkling stars there were some sort of cut gems, and that the moon was a sliver of polished mithra and silver. All around them, ivory-colored pillars stood row on row, carved from bottom to as high as they could see with figures of dwarfish folk and mysterious runes.

In the center of this chamber there was a circular wall about Broco's height, finely wrought of golden stone.

There were no furnishings of any sort, and the smooth, polished floor was empty, and ran on in all directions until the curtain of darkness enveloped it once more, far off in the distance.

"Great beard of Co'in," gasped Dwarf. "It's the Foundation."

He had quickly removed his hat, and bowed twice to the golden wall.

Ned and Cranny, not knowing what else to do, took off their hats, and stood nervously shifting from foot to foot.

Broco walked slowly and reverently to the golden circle and knelt beside it, reaching out a timid hand to touch this most ancient of all dwarfish structures. He was stopped midway by a deep voice from within the dragon stone he held clutched in his small fist.

"Touch not the Foundation. It is only for those who wish to Cross Over."

Dwarf gasped, and jerked his hand back.

"In the first days, it was laid at the heart of Atlanton, below Fairlake, when life was once more given to these worlds. It is a Door to and from Creation."

Cranfallow had leapt to cover behind one of the tall, carven figures as the stone droned on, and Ned simply froze where he stood, eyes bulging.

"Is this what has happened to the lords of old?" asked Dwarf, his voice quavering.

"It is not said how many chose to return this way. But many more were slain, and many forgot this place, and died in the upper realms. And many forgot the Secrets, and perished in the darkness of the world."

As the voice died away, a shining bubble of spun light floated into the stillness, and there, within its glowing form, Dwarf gazed in and saw the histories and lore books repeated in living breath.

He saw the Foundation laid, and the first lords of Dwarfdom, and the beautiful halls they wrought from living stone. And there were untold years that flashed and crossed before him in the span of a breath, then slowly the visions grew more troubled, and at last, a darkness spread across the bright stories, and many disturbed and chaotic scenes followed one after the other.

At the conclusion of a particularly upsetting vision, which had left Dwarf sobbing quietly, and biting his lip to keep from crying aloud, he caught a glimpse of an oddly familiar figure,

neither dwarfish nor elfin kind, arrayed in a
simple gray cloak.

It was some moments before he realized the
figure beckoning to him from within the spun
light was none other than Greyfax Grimwald.

"Greyfax!" he almost shouted, as relief
poured over his aching heart and new hopes
began to flood his mind.

But his hopes were dashed, and his heart fell
when he saw that the wizard was merely speaking to someone within the vision. Fighting back
the despair that had fallen over him, he
struggled against the tears, and peered more
intensely into the spiraling, glowing dome.

Another figure was seated before the wizard,
with his back to Dwarf. There was something
distressingly familiar in that seated shape, and
when it turned so that Broco could see who it
was, he cried aloud again, for it was his own father, just as he had seen him long ago in the
wizard's fire on that first day they had crossed
Calix Stay.

The shimmering, glowing bubble seemed to
brighten, and dazzling blue and red shapes
formed burning outlines of patterns and shapes
in the air around his head, and Broco saw the
dragon stone given to his father, by the hand of
Greyfax.

"Greyfax," called Dwarf aloud, desperately.

And for a moment he thought he saw, or
dreamed he saw, the firm smile of the wizard
turned toward him, saying something he could
not make out.

Before he could puzzle further over the

unheard words, the glowing sphere spun again, and glittering, whirling rainbows of light cast shimmering shadows from the distant dome of the chamber, and a vast array of dwarfish lords passed before his eyes, to fade and vanish in their turn, and at long last, Dwarf saw his own face in the spinning lights, hatless, and wearing a tired frown.

And as quickly as it had come, the glowing bubble of spinning light whirled upon itself and was gone, leaving Dwarf staring hard into the shadows of the far distance of the Foundation Chamber, his fists clenched and his breath coming in shallow, rapid gasps.

Dwarf was startled into the present by a sharp scream from Ned Thinvoice.

"Quick, Cranny. It's them black devils."

Cranfallow's blood ran cold as he looked down the hall to where his friend had wildly pointed.

"We is lost," he groaned, taking a step toward Dwarf.

Broco only sensed the movement at first, so dark were the formless shapes that caught his eye, but he soon saw the crawling blackness that he had mistaken for shadows coil upon themselves and come slithering across the smooth floor of the chamber. He turned, and in a wild moment saw Ned and Cranfallow bolt toward him, and from all four distant corners of the room, the black forms came, silent and awesome in the speed with which they moved.

Dwarf's hand darted to the Chest, but before he could remove it from his cloak, the dragon stone had flamed up once more, and in a voice deep and horrible to hear, had spoken a single, thundering word. Dwarf only half understood it, but knew it to be High Dwarfish, of the ancient lords of Underearth, and for the length of a heartbeat, the black, shapeless things came on, coiling about themselves and smothering the light as they came.

For an instant, Dwarf saw what looked to be horribly formed talons creep forward from the bottom of one of the shapes, the long, sharp claws cruel and wickedly curved. Another bright flash of reddish light leapt up from the dragon stone, and the black shapes became blood-red, with a smoky gray haze above them, and with a blinding roar that exploded into blazing flames, the chamber was filled with shrieking horns and bursting cries, and an endless frenzy of darting forms whirled madly over the heads of the terrified companions.

Great blasts of hot air burnt their eyes, and terrible cries hurt their ears, and misshapen objects flew in searing waves all about them, until at last it seemed the room was caught up in a whirlpool of spinning screams and flashing red lights, spiraling closer and closer to the golden circle in the center, and with one last terrific roar, the lights and noise were swallowed by the open mouth of the Foundation Door, and the three friends were left shaken and dazed, and staring dumbly at each other in a silence so still that it seemed it would most surely go on forever.

THE DRAGON STONE
VANISHES

After what seemed hours, Broco looked down at the dragon stone he still clutched tightly in his fist. It throbbed dimly now, and the light within it had receded far into its depths, and a faint humming sound came from its heart. Dwarf shook himself and stepped back a few paces from the golden well.

"We have seen the last of the Guardians," he said, almost sadly. "It means the ending of these halls, for without them, anyone can loot the treasure rooms, or anything else they like." Broco shook his head in dismay. "Such waste. And after all this time, they should fall prey to the evil."

"I is sure it is a sore, sad stroke of bad luck and all, but that means them things is gone, and that we isn't trapped here no more." Cranfallow breathed a great sigh of relief as he spoke, and the color that had drained from his face now rushed back.

"Hurrah, hurrah," shouted Ned, clapping his friend a great clout on the back, and giving Dwarf a sudden thwack that almost sent the little man tumbling back into the Foundation Well. "Now we is all right, we is, and halfway home."

Broco had aimed a dwarf pummel at Ned, but missed, as Ned danced about.

"Hooorah, and hurrah, we is safe, we is," went on Ned, shouting loudly, making little running leaps and kicking his heels high in the air.

"You is right enough about being out of the clutches of them things that went down that hole," shot Cranny, "but we isn't out of here yet. And we still doesn't have no food or water, and we doesn't know rightly how we is going to find a door to gets out, even if them things is all gone back wherever it is they come from."

At the mention of food, Ned cooled down quickly, and became more solemn. "Well, we is alive to fret about it, anyhows," he grumbled, looking a bit sheepish.

Broco had said nothing, and after picking up the dragon stone, which he had let drop when Ned jostled him, he cleared his throat and spoke in a somewhat subdued manner. "We must bear east from here," he said slowly, "for the Foundation was laid in the very heart of the kingdom of Co'in, in the First Beginning. I have read of the histories of these halls as a young spanner, and know we are below all the

other realms of these halls. Deeper than ever
mine or shaft of Dwarfdom was the Foundation, and so we have a long march ahead of us
to reach the upper levels, or any portal that
goes up to the outside."

"How long is far?" asked Cranfallow, his
voice anxious.

"A long way," replied Dwarf.

From his memory he called up the stories of
this chamber and the journey to it, and he
knew they had little hope of reaching even the
lowest level of the upper halls without food or
water. And between here and the shaft that led
upward to any of the upper halls was the Under Tide. But he said nothing of this.

"Well, we ought to start doing a little more
with our feet than standing on them. Sooner
doing, sooner done, I always says," said Ned,
patiently straightening his cloak and preparing
to do whatever was to be done.

"I stands with Ned on that," said Cranfallow.
"But you know, it weren't no eyes of many men
what's ever seen the likes of all that." His eyes
went wide in awe, and his hand circled around
his head a few times to indicate the furious ac-
tivity of a moment before.

"Why, you is right as rain there, Cranny. It
were something to tear the breath right out of
you, it were. I like to have swallowed my
tongue, I did. All them shrieks and goings-on
fair stood up my hackles, I don't mind saying."

"Our Dwarf sure knows what he's about, fair
and proper. And we is most proud to be with

you, sir," said Cranny grandly, giving Broco
the benefit of a wide, rather toothless smile.

"I'm honored, I'm sure, good Cranny and
Ned. But we must make a start from here. It's
going to be weary going, and I think we should
save our breath for the walking." Dwarf forced
himself to speak casually.

"Lead on then, Master Dwarf. We is sore
ready to see a piece of daylight with these old
eyes," said Ned jovially. The bad fright and escape had made him feel giddy.

As the friends had been talking, a steady
hum had gone on in a low, droning sound that
now became louder. Dwarf realized it was coming from the dragon stone, and he held it up to
look more closely at the pale silver fire that now
shone in its shadowy depths.

As he peered more closely, a small scene un-
folded in the shimmering stone that left him
stunned with horror. There, in the heart of the
stone, was the image of himself, hurling the
dragon stone into the golden deepness of the
Foundation.

"No," he muttered, "I can't. We've no light
but yours. And you're all the aid we have in
this place."

Ned and Cranny stood silently as Dwarf
went on talking to the faintly glowing object he
held before him.

The humming grew stronger, and the voice
of the stone rose in a faint tone.

"The time has come as was foretold. You
have carried me long and well, and my task

upon Atlanton is done. I would now return to
my own rest."

The hum grew fainter, and the light dimmed
until the outlines of the stone's depths were
barely visible.

"But how are we to go on from here?" asked
Dwarf in a choked voice.

"You will find what you need in the Musical
Room," came the reply. "And now, farewell,
Broco, last lord of Underearth of these silent
halls. It was so written."

With a spluttering flash, the dragon stone
flared briefly with a silver-white flame, then
went dark. All Dwarf now held was a com-
mon-looking gray stone, cold to the touch.

"Then farewell, old friend. May your rest be
long and refreshing," he cried, and hurled the
silent stone into the golden mouth of the well.

A far-off rumble erupted from the smooth
floor beneath them, and a hot wind seemed to
spring up from the very walls, then quietened
again. The rumbling tremor went on for quite
some time.

"Is it a earth shake?" trembled Ned, looking
wildly about him.

"No, I think not, Ned. It was the stone."

Before Broco finished speaking, the last faint
glimmering of light in the tall chamber whirled
twice about the room and swept into the mouth
of the golden well. They were in total darkness
once more.

"A fine mess of stuff we is in now," complained Ned bitterly. "Just like them magical
things to up and leave a fellow when he needs

them most." Ned's misgivings about the nature of all mysterious powers returned in full force.

"If I remember rightly," said Dwarf, paying no attention to his friend, "we bear left from here, until we come to the chamber the stone spoke of." His voice lowered, and he went on. "And that level is before the water," he said, half aloud.

But his hopes had returned with the words from the dragon stone, and he went on more cheerfully. "The Musical Room was a splendid place, from all I've read. The very walls sang, and all sorrows were eased by listening to those songs there."

"Well, it's a sure thing we isn't going to be able to see it," muttered Ned, "so leastways I hope we is able to hear it when we gets there."

"Buck up, Ned," scolded Cranfallow. "We isn't lost, leastways. We heard what that fellow in the rock said."

"That's all fine and proper, for the likes of him, I reckon. He don't have to worry about getting a drink, or barking his shins, or getting up a bite to gnaw on."

"We'll see the sooner what it meant, I think," said Dwarf, half huffing, "if we get there first."

"That's for plumb sure," agreed Cranny. "And old Ned here loves to see the black side of everything that comes his lot. It's just his way."

"I is sure seeing the black side to this business," grumbled Ned. "If you could say I was seeing at all."

"Here, take hold of my cloak, Cranny. Ned,

you hold to Cranny," said Dwarf. "The quicker we're there, the sooner we'll find out what the stone meant."

Cranfallow took the hem of the cloak Dwarf held out to him, and still muttering to himself, Ned grabbed Cranfallow's cloak roughly, and the three set off once more, going slowly, and stopping every few steps so that Dwarf could check his direction.

They had gone on in this way for a half hour or more, when the soft, muted sound of music began to reach them, low and muffled, and difficult to make out, but music such as they had never heard before. Immediately they all felt heartened, and went forward at a faster pace. Dwarf no longer halted to make sure of his way, and soon all three were jogging along blindly in the flat, empty blackness that hung heavily about them.

IN THE MUSICAL ROOM

Ahead, against the darker outline of shadows, Dwarf could make out what looked to be a deep blue hole against the blackness beyond it.

Ned, plodding along beside Broco, broke into a low gasp of relief. "It's there, right enough. Old Ned's eyes ain't what they was afore we got stuck in this hole, but they is good enough to see a light what's there."

"I sees it, too," broke in Cranny. "All blue like."

The three slowed to a walk, and began noticing their surroundings, barely visible in the shaded blue glow that filtered out of the opening ahead. Tall shadows with many queer shapes loomed out of the darkness against the wall. Ned cried out a warning when his eyes caught the dim, dreadful shapes, but Dwarf only laughed.

"It's water pots, or the like. And look, there's a larder chest."

Cranfallow broke into a trot, and raised himself on tiptoe to look into a tall urn formed in the shape of a huge horse with the head of an elf.

"It's something that smells powerful good," he said. "Almost like sniffing a flower."

"It's from the river that flows through here," explained Dwarf. "It was said to be the sweetest water in Atlanton Earth."

"But how does we get at it?" asked Cranny. "It's too tall to dip out."

"Here," said Dwarf, striding to stand in front of the urn. "The spout is the bowl the hands are holding."

He touched the outstretched hand of the figure, and the finely wrought bowl was suddenly overflowing with the sweet-smelling water. Cranfallow and Thinvoice splashed noisily in the cool wetness, and soaked their kerchiefs in it and wiped their faces and necks. During their makeshift bath they took long gulps of the water's refreshing clearness, and felt the new strength surge through them.

Dwarf sensed a change almost immediately after his long drink, and found he had forgotten how thirsty he had been. The awakening in the woods of Garius, and the fight at the ruins, and all in-between had almost slipped from his mind, almost as if it had never happened. It seemed as if they had been in these halls forever, so slowly had the time passed in the darkness, and after the freeing of the Guardi-

ans and the return of the dragon stone to the
Foundation, all time was lost to him, and he
had no idea whether it was day or night beyond
these ancient chambers. And sweeping over him
in a flood of sorrow and sadness was the separa-
tion from Otter and Bear.

"A fine fix I've gotten us to," he muttered to
himself. "Most likely they're stuck somewhere in
the Dragur, or lost in the Dragon Wastes, cursing the day they ever laid eyes on a dwarf."

"Who is?" called Ned, wiping his face again
with his damp neck cloth.

"Bear, and Otter, and Flewingam," answered
Dwarf, stepping back from the water urn and
drying his mouth with his cloak.

Cranfallow stopped in the middle of another
long drink. "I has forgotten all about the poor
blighters, I has," he said remorsefully, and
stood up shaking his head. "A fine friend I is,
lapping up water like a dog while our friends is
most likely as not parched as a bone somewheres."

"We might try taking one of these here water
jugs with us, so's if we runs into 'em, they could
has a drink, too," suggested Ned.

"No, Ned. We couldn't carry one of these.
Not without horses or carts."

"Then what is we going to do?" asked Ned,
eyeing the heavy water urn. "We can't stays
here."

"Not long, nohow," put in Cranny. "Not if
we is going to reach the outside."

Broco fell into a long silence, thinking hard
and screwing up his face into a small frown.

Ned and Cranfallow looked at each other, and remained silent. Dwarf startled them both by suddenly driving his fist into his palm.

"Bother it all, and dwarf curses on it," he stammered. "How am I to leave my friends in this flummox? I have to bear the Chest until someone takes it, but no one's been stumbling over their feet to get at it except that foul sister of Lorini's. And I'm not even sure beyond this room of where we are, much less how to get us over Calix Stay. Or even if we can get across if we get there."

Broco stumped off a few paces, then returned, his small face drawn into a scowl.

"Well, you does have them powers," offered Ned, a little sheepishly.

"Dwarf tricks to amuse spanners," snorted Dwarf angrily, "and certainly nothing to deal with the likes of this."

"But they has stood us in good stead more than once, sir," interrupted Cranfallow. "And we'd be a sore bit worse off it we wasn't with you in this dungeon."

"I'm not so sure, Cranny. If you weren't tangled up with the likes of me, as like as not you'd be safe somewhere with General Greymouse now, at a job you're more familiar with."

"Well, I wouldn't go so far as all that, now. We might be with the general, right enough, wherever he is. But I don't know as how we'd be a smidgen better off. Things was taking a terrible turn when we run into you again. Lughs and Lacs all over, and our own troops getting fewer all the while. Them isn't odds what I'd call square."

"And likes it or not, we doesn't ever suffer no time squatting too long at one post," added Ned. "And if I remembers rightly, we was mumbling in our stew about that when we first got sight of you, when we was up toward them wildland borders." Ned flushed as he spoke, and stood looking at his feet.

"You've both served me better than I could ask," said Dwarf more gently, "and stood by me where others would have given over."

"We ain't done nothing of the sort," began Cranny, but Dwarf cut him short.

"And I want to say I'm proud to be in the company of such stout comrades. You've earned a fairer reward than I shall ever be able to pay you."

"Bosh," spluttered Ned, turning a deeper red. "We is only adoing what we is able. And that don't seem like no overly lot."

As Ned fell silent, the music that had been going on all the while changed timbre and grew slightly louder.

Cranfallow had noticed it before the others, and had been listening intently. "Hush!" he whispered, and Dwarf and Ned looked questioningly at him, then heard the new melody that vibrated through the silence of the walls.

"It's trying to say something," said Cranny, "only I can't quite makes out the words."

Broco stepped quickly to the smooth surface of the cool stones of the wall and placed his ear close to it.

He remained there for a long time, listening. And when he at last leaned away from the mirrored finish, his face wore a puzzled expression.

"I can't make much of it out," he said, "other than something to do with roots, or some such."

"Roots?" snorted Ned.

"And something else about the river Under Tide."

"Must be some old dwarfish ditty, I guess," said Cranny, disappointed with the news, for the song had somehow sounded more important.

"Yet there is an underground river through this realm, or was of old. It was used as a highway before the day came that the lords of Underearth sealed off their kingdoms from outside eyes." Dwarf paused, thinking hard. "But I never heard of anything mentioning roots. I know of the Guardians, and their task, and have seen the end of them. But roots?"

"I hope they isn't like them last things," shuddered Ned. "They was enough to plumb stand the hair on your head stiff out."

"I can't say, Ned. Although it kept coming over and over," said Dwarf, and he broke into a snatch of song.

"The Roots will meet at Under Tide
     with those of old,
          from Overside,
               and as a gift for those
                    who come from far away,
               The Roots
                    will give them
                         light of day."

"Don't make much sense, do it?" said Ned, scratching his head.

Dwarf's face suddenly brightened. "The stone said I would have something to help me here. And I don't think it meant just finding the water."

"Does you think there is some grub handy, too?" asked Cranny.

"More than that, don't you see? This must have something to do with the song. It must be a message of some sort."

"But they ain't no river hereabouts, or we woulda heard it."

"True, Ned. But the river is farther up than this. Much farther."

"Then how is we going to get there? We still doesn't have no grub. And we can't tote no water with us."

"Come on," said Dwarf, turning and rushing deeper into the soft blue light of the Musical Room. "We'll make a closer inspection here."

Ned and Cranny had to trot to keep up with the sturdy strides of Dwarf. They went on through tier after tier of the many-shaped water urns, which seemed to line the walls of the entire chamber. And more toward the center of the room, they saw low, carven couches, and chairs, and small tables with what looked to be cups upon them. Dwarf cast a hasty glance about the immense hall and strode on, Ned and Cranfallow hurrying along behind, casting doubtful looks at each other.

Cranfallow was on the verge of asking Broco to slow his pace when Dwarf called out in an excited voice. "I thought as much," he cried. "The storehouses."

Ned and Cranfallow broke into a brisk trot and soon stood beside Dwarf.

"They always kept these at various levels," explained Broco, "in case they were set upon and forced to withdraw farther in. This one looks well stocked."

And the room did overflow with all manner of equipment and gear, hanging off the walls and stacked high in piles about the floor. There was a vast array of ancient dwarfish armor and weapons, from pike to sturdy dwarf ax, and short swords, shields, bucklers, and daggers, along with stubby bows and quivers of wicked-looking barbed arrows.

Their eyes scanned these weapons hurriedly, and fell upon what they were more in need of. In stout oaken casks, Dwarf had found what he had sought.

"Journey cakes," said Dwarf triumphantly, and pried open one of the heavy chests.

Inside were oiled and layered rows of the dwarf staples, all baked in the shape of a hammer and stored in the ancient manner of dwarfs. He reached in gently and placed a finger to a cake, and cried out in delight.

"Leave it to well-made dwarf cake. They last forever."

Ned, who had peeked in over Dwarf's shoulder, made a face and gritted his teeth. "That's all well enough, but I doesn't has no taste for stale biscuit."

Dwarf drew out his small knife and cut one

of the cakes. He handed a piece to Ned, and another to Cranny, and gulped down the bit he had cut for himself.

"Why, I reckon this ain't half so bad as gnawing on a piece of rock, Ned. Not half bad at all."

Thinvoice, with his mouth full, managed a grunt in agreement.

When the three friends had satisfied their hunger for the moment, and they were far hungrier than they had thought, they sat down upon the food cask and looked about them at the vast array of arms there.

"I don't think we'll find much of anything here that will be of use to us," said Dwarf, stooping and picking up a broad-headed ax. "It would be one thing to sort through this lot to study the histories of these halls, but quite another to find anything we could use against a troop of Gorgolacs or Worlughs."

"At least I has a stomach that ain't ahounding me to death," sighed Ned contentedly. "And we might be out of range of them Lacs or Lughs. We doesn't know where we is, rightly. So we isn't in no real need of nothing to fights with. Leastways, not down here."

"If it's out of the reach of them filth, then we has come a fair piece for sure. I didn't know there was no place that they wasn't."

"We may or may not be beyond the enemȳ, but I would feel easier if I had something to at least make me feel better," said Dwarf, testing the heft of the sturdy dwarf ax.

"That's right scary itself, sir," said Cranny.

"And I remember you was after stirring up a spell like at Seven Hills, and them dwarfs was all carrying them axes just like that there."

Dwarf laughed. Seven Hills was an almost forgotten tale, just at the edge of his memory.

"You remember well, Cranny. I think, then, I shall carry it, for luck. If it's not much good for cleaving heads, I might at least use it to chop firewood."

"Things doesn't seem to get old none down here at all. Look at this," called Ned, who was waist-deep in a pile of leather equipment of some fashion. He held up a leather shirt that was still dark and soft. "And this." Another dark, smooth leather object.

"And that, my friend, is a find," shouted Dwarf, making a little leap over a stack of oiled and stacked short swords.

"Water bottles, good friends, and sturdy packs, that we may carry some rations away with us."

After another search, they found more of the soft skin water bottles and rucksacks among the stacks and piles of the ancient gear.

"I guess sodjers is sodjers, for all that," said Ned, loading one of the packs with dwarf cakes. "It don't seem like they was any different back then than they is now. Still a pack is a pack, and has to have a back to tote it."

"And a sore one, what's to boot," laughed Cranny. "Armies is the only things what don't get old and die, curse the luck."

"I'm going to fill up some of these skins with water, Ned. You pack as many of those as we

can carry, and then some. Cranny, you help me
with these bottles."

"Does you think it'll be safe enough for a nap
when we is done?" asked Cranny as he walked
beside Broco to the water urns.

"I was just thinking of a nap myself, good
Cranny. When we've supplied ourselves, we'll
make what plans as we may, and take ourselves
some well-earned rest."

"That's the most welcome news I has heard
since I found out old Ned wasn't done up at
Seven Hills."

The two friends fell silent, quickly filled the
skins as full as they could, and dragged them
back to where they had left Ned packing the
food.

"Here now, where has Neddy got off to?"
asked Cranny.

Dwarf's heart pounded wildly, and he cursed
himself for his carelessness at thinking they
were safe for the moment in the ancient halls of
his ancestors. They raced into the room, Dwarf
brandishing the sturdy dwarf ax, and Cranfallow with his dagger drawn, eyes wild and filled
with battle fire. On the floor amid the heap of
jumbled equipment they found Ned, his head
fallen against a full rucksack that he had been
packing. He was lying very still.

"What hurt has he?" cried Dwarf, glaring
about him, seeking whatever foe had found
them.

A rasping noise came from behind, and he
whirled, holding the deadly-looking ax high
above his head.

"I guess the only hurt he has is no sleep," grinned Cranfallow foolishly. "He's out cold as a fish."

Broco slowly lowered his terrible ax, and stood dazed as the moment of danger passed. "Well, by the beard," he yawned at last. "I guess that's what we all need."

And lying down beside Cranny, the two friends tucked up rough leather pillows for their heads, and covered themselves with their cloaks.

"Does you think there is any need to one of us staying on guard?" asked Cranfallow drowsily.

"Even if there was a need, I don't think we would be able to do it," Dwarf replied with a long, fluttering sigh, and began to snore peacefully.

Soon the armory rang with the unfamiliar sound of snoring and sleepy snorts.

And Dwarf, in a dream, if dream it was, stood looking at the immense dome of the Foundation Room. Before him was the golden well, the stairway to the upper regions, and in a glimmering pale sheen of brilliant white light stood a dwarf, scowling slightly, and motioning Broco to step closer. His heart stopped, for as the bright light dimmed, he saw the strange dwarf was none other than Eo'in himself, the father of all dwarfish kind across Creation, the architect of these sacred dwarf-wrought halls, and the setter of the Foundation Stone.

"Sire," breathed Broco, falling to one knee.

"Welcome, brother Broco, Bearer of the Arkenchest, Lore Master. My hopes have been well met, and my name always honored in your heart."

"Yes, sire," muttered Dwarf, unable to take his eyes away from the glimmering figure.

"You have come to an end of a prophecy here, you and your friends. It was written long ago that these ancient halls would return to their beginning at the return of dwarfish folk. We have seen the release of the Guardians, and the cracking of the Foundation. Now the Under Tide is raging, and ready to fulfill its destiny."

"Destiny, sire?" asked Dwarf.

"Yes, fate, good spanner. The Under Tide is to wipe clean the existence of all this, and the very mountain we dwell under. It is to return all to newness. And we have played out our part as was meant. Now you come, signaling the final act."

"I, sire?"

"Your appearance has been long noted, and the Council of Elders has watched your progress through all these lives, following on down until this moment. It was written that the Delvings and Foundation shall be taken back by the Bearer of the Secrets. And now we shall all have done our part in this Creation, for Dwarfkind, along with all other kind, has completed its mission upon Atlanton Earth, and now may find rest in the warmth of Home."

Blazing blue-white stars exploded across Broco's vision, and a raging torrent of flaming spheres melted into a towering, unbearable light that reached away until all color flowed into its brilliance. Broco covered his eyes and fell forward, covering his face with his hands. He felt frightened, yet bursting with joy.

"Come and see, my brother," came a voice that was yet not a voice.

Dwarf looked up, and as he watched in stunned amazement, Eo'in's form began to undergo a transformation. Silver mist covered Eo'in, and after the air had cleared, a figure appeared that caused Dwarf to cry out in wonder and amazement.

"Greyfax. It's you. Oh, thank the Foundation you've come for the Chest," Dwarf blurted out, the tears of joy and relief pouring forth from him.

"No, my dear friend, not Greyfax, yet the same. Names are only things of convenience, and often change. And I have not come for the Chest. I rather come to give you hope, and say that you are very close to your crossing of Calix Stay. As it turns out, your friend the dragon stone is responsible for your return to beyond the River. The Under Tide and the moving of the Roots shall free you from this plane, and allow you onto the next, where you will carry on your task of bearing the Chest."

"But all I'm supposed to do is return it across Calix Stay. Then I shall be free of it," said Dwarf slowly. "Or that's what I was led to believe. I can't go on with this much longer. It is too heavy for the likes of me to bear."

"I know, my dear friend. But it is only you who may bear it now. All else hinges upon the

Arkenchest arriving across the Borders in your hands. And it is already so written."

"Couldn't you take it now?" asked Broco hopefully.

"I cannot. It is only mine to deliver to you these words, and to tell you of your crossing."

"Can't you tell me more, or what I'm to do once I get across? Or tell Greyfax for me, or get Froghorn? I'm so tired, and I've lost my friends, and nothing has turned out right since I've returned here this time."

"The others of the Circle know your whereabouts, Broco. Froghorn even yet awaits you. And your friends are not far from you, even at this moment. But that is all I need say for now. Good heart and stout spirit, my friend. And keep your faith in the Light."

All faded, and Dwarf started awake with a sob, to the incessant tune he had heard from the walls of the Music Chamber, and it seemed as if it had grown louder, and nearer, but he could not tell if the dream had been but a dream, or real.

And below, far beneath the dwarf and his friends, a Root and his companions halted at the rugged edge of the roaring waters of the river called Under Tide.

THE UNDER TIDE

"Where sea and sky
  and earth are one,
    there is the door
      to Under Tide,
  raging waters from the depths
    use the sunlight
      as its steps."

So spoke the Root Kore.

"Ahem," began Bear, clearing his throat and looking uneasily at the frothing rapids of the water.

Kore's eyes were open, and that eerie light reflected off the rushing torrent before them.

"Thank you, I'm sure," went on Bear. "And it's certainly reassuring knowing we're here and all, and that this river leads to somewhere outside. But what I'm wondering," he said, pausing for a moment, looking at Otter and

Thumb, "is how we're going to make use of this?"

Otter had crept to the very brink of the roaring flood, and sniffed and pawed it cautiously. His whiskers stiffened, and he stirred a quick paw through the foaming water that eddied about the sloping sides of the bank, which was also stone, and appeared to have been a regular quay at one time, when it was younger, for great iron rings for mooring boats of some fashion still showed their rusty hoops in the gloom of Kore's dim-lighted eyes.

"It feels all right," called Otter to the others, after puttering around a few moments longer. "And it smells all right. I'm sure it's good water."

"Good for what, without a craft?" asked Flewingam. "None of us are the swimmer you are, friend. We couldn't last a second in that, and if we could, we'd have to leave our clothes and whatever else here."

"He's right, Otter. It might be well enough for you or me or Flewingam, but we have Thumb's company to think of. I don't think the little ones could last." Bear ambled forward as he spoke, and stood beside Otter, although not quite so close to the tumbling rapids of the river.

"I'm afraid I wouldn't be able to swim this very well," mused Otter, his gray face working into a frown. "Much too swift. Be beaten against a rock and drowned, as likely as not."

"Are there any sort of boats left here, Kore, from the old days?" asked Flewingam.

"The hollow things of old are all perished, eaten by the earth, or gone with those that built them," boomed the Root's reply.

"Is there anything along this old quay we could use to fashion a raft, I wonder?" asked Flewingam, who paced ahead into the darker shadows, studying the floor of the cavern.

"Let's spread out and see," suggested Bear. "We'll go this way a bit, and you go that. But don't go out of hailing distance."

"Will you wait a while longer with us, Kore?" asked Thumb. "I'm afraid we don't see well without your help."

"Kore abides forever," boomed the Root. "I have time enough to wait somewhat longer, although I begin to think of my feed."

"Oh, thank you," crooned Lilly, wanting to give the Root a bear hug, but not sure at all how one would go about it.

Thumb gathered her hurriedly up, and with the rest of his band, set off slowly down the side of the landing they were to search. He had gone no more than a dozen bear paces when he stumbled and fell foward onto his forepaws.

"Owwwww," he moaned, turning and rubbing his stubbed hind leg. "What's that?"

All the others had circled him and sat looking at the odd-shaped thing that had caused him to fall. It was a ring of some sort, shaped like the outline of a small skiff, although it took them a moment to make it out, for it was very rusty. And none of them had ever seen a rowing skiff, and no one knew exactly what to make of it.

"I guess they put it there so someone would get bumped on it," offered Lilly, running her paws over the rusted, rough surface of it.

"Maybe some of the others know," said Thumb, and called as loudly as he could to make himself heard over the roaring water.

Otter, who was nearest, heard him cry out, and galloped clumsily back to the ring of bears.

"What is it?" he shouted, thinking they had discovered something of a sort they could build a raft with.

"What is this?" asked Thumb, pointing with a blunt forepaw at the odd thing in the center of the group.

Otter peered, then pawed the thing, smelled, pawed, and looked more closely. "I guess it's only a mooring ring," he said at last, his voice disappointed.

"What's that?" asked Lilly.

"A thing you tie a boat to," explained Otter rather shortly.

"Oh, I see," said Lilly, who had no idea what he was talking about.

"But look here, it's almost come out of the stone," said Storm. "See, the whole thing is tilted."

Otter looked again, putting his muzzle very close to the floor, and putting his nose right up against the block, which had somehow shifted. "It smells funny. There's something under it. The air is all different. Sort of, oh, musty like."

Bear and Flewingam had rejoined their friends after finding nothing of use in their search.

"Is it something, Otter? A board, or barrel?" asked Flewingam, crowding in among the others.

"It's something, but I'm not sure what."

"Let me see it," said Flewingam, and he knelt beside the rusted ring. With a small cry, he leaned forward after a moment and began pulling with all his strength on the iron rung. "It's a trapdoor," he grunted, straining his arms against the weight of the stone. "Here, catch hold, and help me."

Bear lumbered up, and seeing what was needed, put his powerful forepaws around the handle, and blowing hard, put all his great strength into play. A tiny crack appeared as the huge stone moved the slightest bit. With another great tug, the ring snapped with a report like a rifle shot, and Bear, not expecting the sudden release, tumbled backward off-balance, tripped over the startled Otter, and with a last bellow of surprise and terror fell with a great splash into the foaming rapids a few steps beyond. Before anyone could gather his senses or make a move, Bear's last call had been drowned in the rushing torrent.

Stunned, and staring in disbelief at the raging white-capped flood before them, Otter broke into a choking sob, and if Flewingam had not grabbed him firmly by the shoulder, he would have leapt in after his vanished friend.

Lilly was crying in long, wailing sobs, and all the other bears shuffled their forepaws slowly and shook their great heads in time to a low, rumbling, growling song.

Otter squirmed and struggled to free himself from Flewingam's grasp.

"I have to go after him," he sobbed. "The clumsy lummox can't swim in that. Why, he can't wade, without half drowning himself."

"Leave it, friend," said Flewingam gently. "It's no good."

"I have to try," wailed Otter, wriggling harder, trying to repeat the spell that would give him his human form.

Flewingam held him more firmly. "He's gone, friend. But perhaps he can swim ashore farther down. We'll follow along the bank and see if we can find him."

"It was my fault," choked Otter. "He fell over me. I'm a clumsy, stupid animal, and I've been the death of my dearest friend."

"Hold, Otter. It was no fault of yours. He fell by accident," comforted Flewingam.

"But we'd better get on. He may have need of us." Thumb placed a gentle forepaw on Otter's shoulder.

"Not likely in this world," said Otter bitterly.

"Then we must look to getting Thumb and the others out. You know Bear would not have deserted his friends in their need."

Otter's face screwed up in an effort to stem his tears. He coughed, and cleared his throat twice, and spoke in a trembling voice. "Then fair is fair. I shall see to it you get all the help I am able to give until we reach the outside. Then I shall come back alone, and go on with my search for Bear."

Flewingam said no more, but released Otter,

and the despondent group set out slowly in single file beside the swift gray current of the river.

Every few yards, Thumb would look at the boiling water racing by, and say in a hopeful tone, "There's many places here he could hang onto, or pull himself out on. I'm sure he's a stout swimmer, and he's strong. He may be waiting for us just ahead there. I think I can see a place where the water is quieter."

But the kind words left Otter unmoved, and he stalked along as if in a dream, looking straight ahead, or sobbing quietly into his paws.

After a few more minutes, the booming voice of the Root rang out in dull tones against the loud noise of the rushing water. "Kore is too near the top to stay, he must return to his own."

"We can't see without your eyes," protested Flewingam. "Can't you stay with us just a bit longer?"

"You are welcome to stay with the Roots," Kore boomed, "but I can go no farther. I already feel weakened in this light air."

"Let him go," said Otter flatly. "We can go on as well in the dark. We just have to keep to the water." He turned and bowed to the Root. "Many thanks for your aid. I shall return to stay with you once we have found the way out for the others."

"As you wish, oh, traveler on the Under Tide. We are the Roots, we abide forever. May your roots grow deeper," boomed Kore, and without further word, the light blinked out, and the ground trembled and rippled, and they were alone in the dark once more.

THE MOUNTAINS OF BEGINNING

▩ A wild, wet, roaring noise broke all around Bear's spinning head. He fought desperately with a giant hand that tried to pull him under the frothing waters, and struggled to keep his muzzle pointed above its cresting tide. He made a brief, vain effort at trying to swim out of it, to where he thought the bank would be, but quickly realized it would be all he could do to keep his head above water.

Panic overtook him for a moment, and the flood pulled him under the dark, churning surface, its relentless grip dragging him deeper into its cold belly, until at last, with one gasping, choking struggle that was more than he thought he could do, he resurfaced, spluttering, with his lungs on fire, paddling wildly on top of the raging torrent.

He felt himself catapulted along faster and faster, until at last it seemed he was flying over

the top of the churning waters, and he found
that as long as he kept himself in an upright
position, he could keep his head free, and
breathe. Once he felt himself touch bottom, but
the relentless current bore him on before he
could manage to free himself, and he scraped
himself painfully in trying to stand on the slippery surface of the stream bed.

On and on he went, washed by the angry
river, until after a time, he began to tire and to
be afraid he would faint and drown. His limbs
ached and pulled him down like weights, and
he could not tell if he were moving them or if it
was only a trick of his mind. For what seemed
like days he struggled numbly on, keeping his
head just above water, and trying to keep himself from passing out with fatigue.

He had been repeating his friends' names,
and gone on to listing the trees he knew in the
different woods he had dwelled in, and was beginning to go over the various types of honey,
when he heard himself, as if it were not his
voice at all, repeat the spell that gave him his
man form. He forgot the middle words at first
and puzzled over that a moment or two, but in
the next breath he felt new strength surge
through him, and felt his numbed limbs rea-
wakened in their new form.

For the first time in what seemed hours, he
began to try to find someplace to swim out of
the raging stream, and he realized, with a
shocked awareness, that he was able to make
out shapes and shadows, and that all was no

longer the unending darkness, and roar of the water.

If there had been boulders or stones in the bed of the swift-running current, he would have been knocked senseless and drowned, he knew. But there was only a smooth surface beneath his feet, on the times he had been able to touch it, and he found he was able to touch it now each time he put out his legs and stretched. This renewed his hopes, and he began carefully to prepare himself for an all-out effort to swim free of the surging current.

The river channel appeared to bend slightly ahead, and Bear gathered his strength to make his bid for freedom. The light had grown steadily, until it seemed almost unbearably bright to his dark-seeing eyes, but he was unprepared for the next instant, when he was swept clear of the bend in the channel bed and flung bodily into an exploding white sunlight that burst inside his head like cannon fire, and dazzling, sparkling water flew upward in towering, shining spumes of spray, whirling away upward in searing silver flashes.

Bear had to shut his eyes tightly, but the lights went on, and he felt a wild, spinning motion suck him up to a dizzying, terrifying height, and he seemed to whirl there suspended forever. Great crashing noises exploded all about him, and a voice, or a chorus of voices, roared out of the whirling waters, but he could not make out the words. He was bumped and banged with things that spun in the wild dance beside him, and he sensed that some of these

things were disappearing, one by one. And
then he heard the voices speak his name, his
old name, Biarki, son of Algunner, and he understood them clearly this time.

He was weak with fright, and exhausted, but
he heard himself answering in his turn. He
could not have spoken anything but the truth,
even if he had wished to. He flashed and
whirled in a spiraling sheet of water that
howled like wind-driven spirits and glistened
like blazing sheets of silver fire. And all the
while, his own voice went on, never ceasing,
telling of his crossing of Calix Stay so long ago,
and his travels with Broco and Otter, through
the easy years in the fair valley, to Dwarf's capture by the Darkness, and the journey to find
General Greymouse, and Seven Hills, and Cypher, and the lady Lorini, and on to the leaving of Cypher once more, and the battle upon
Hel and Havamal, and the search for the
Chest, and finding it, and the struggle to get
the Chest once more across the River, where it
would be safe, and Greyfax, or Froghorn, or
Melodias, could once more take charge of it.

As suddenly as it had all begun, the wild tor-
rents of silver fire subsided, and he floated
along in a glowing darkness, in utter silence.
His ears rang, and he was still dizzy from the
whirling wind he had been trapped in a moment before, and he had a brief moment of biting self-reproach when he recalled all he had
said. If he were in the hands of the Dark
Queen, he would have been the undoing of all

his friends and the Circle, and the betrayer of
the Arkenchest.

But this feeling passed almost at once, and
he knew he was not at the mercy of any enemy.
As his reeling thoughts cleared and he became
calmer, he detected a faint, faraway light
growing, as if he were seeing a sunrise over a
vast range of high mountains. Then he realized
that he was very high up, above a distant
forest, with golden yellow fields running up to
its edge, and small white clouds were scudding
along below him.

Before he could think about that, he seemed
to be rushing headlong into a long, thin, dark
blue ribbon that wound through the golden
fields, and he suddenly felt the cool, damp
splash of water once more, gurgling all about
him.

He flailed out wildly, thinking he was still
caught in the roaring current of the underground river, and he spluttered and struggled,
and tried to swim free of its pull. To his very
great surprise, he found himself lying on his
stomach in a cool, trickling stream that flowed
gently over pebbles of many hues and colors, of
reds and fiery coppers, and blues and greens,
and the water formed quietly gurgling pools
beside low, grass-covered banks that were only
a few paces across.

He sat up in amazement, and looked at his
surroundings more closely. They seemed familiar, yet changed in some way. He stood awk-
wardly, and remembered, after looking down
at himself, that he was in his man form.

"Well," he stammered, feeling at once like laughing, or crying. "Well, for the life of me," he blurted out, and stumbled onto the soft grass of the bank and sat down wearily, and had a small, hiccuping sobbing bout.

After he had gotten his breath and looked around once more, he repeated the words to the spell Froghorn had given them on a morning so long ago it was now dimmed in his memory. He said them slowly, and with great care, but to his dismay, he remained in his man form. He went through the whole spell again, with the same results, looking down in utter amazement at the hands that remained where his great forepaws should have appeared, and at a loden green vest, where the white-colored fur should have blended into the reddish-brown fur of his chest.

After a number of attempts, he gave up sadly.

"I've probably forgotten one of the words," he said aloud, and cheered himself up with the thought that he would remember it as soon as his ordeal had worn off somewhat and he was more himself.

To take his mind off trying to remember the spell, he set out to explore the oddly familiar place he found himself so abruptly thrust into. Away to his right, a tall stand of oak and beech trees began, and farther downstream, he saw the first of many pools the watercourse made on its long journey. They went on and on, until they seemed to meet the horizon. And there he saw the dim, hazy outlines of a mountain range, pale blue in the immense distance. His heart stirred within him, and a wild excitement washed over him, although he could not think why. He walked forward a few steps, shaded his eyes, and peered a long time at the distant humps of the mountains' backs.

He was still staring at the far-distant forms when another, more familiar noise jerked him from his thoughts. The sound of horses, and men afoot, and the jingle and clink of pack gear reached him. And for the first time, he realized he had been hearing another sound for quite some minutes without registering what it was.

The dull thud and whump of heavy mortars and cannon fire, booming away at a great distance, flooded his mind suddenly, and without thinking further, he was racing for the cover of the nearby wood.

BEYOND EVEN DREAMS

▨ Bear had gone only a few steps when overhead he heard a high, buzzing whine whistle by him, and the memory of those sounds was buried very deeply. The rifle report came faintly, away somewhere behind him, followed by others, and the small geysers of dirt he remembered well from Seven Hills began erupting all around him, and the ugly crackling noise of bullets as they tore through the still air buzzed and roared all about him.

He was breathing hard and crouched almost double as he fell behind the broad trunk of a low-branched tree. Rolling over quickly, Bear looked back at his pursuers, far away, but now closing the distance rapidly, firing as they came.

Bear squinted, trying to catch his breath and discover who these enemies were. He could make out dull gray helmets and what looked to

be gray tunics and uniforms. They weren't the
misshapen Worlughs or Gorgolacs, so they had
to be men. And the leader of the squad that
came toward him was mounted on a copper-
colored horse that danced and threw his head
about, flaring his great nostrils and straining at
his bit. Bear could make out no markings on
any of the uniforms, and other than that they
were all gray, he could detect nothing. Yet they
were shooting at him, and closing the distance
quickly.

He looked behind him and saw the thin
wood thickened a few hundred paces or so farther, and without waiting any longer, or wondering who these strange new enemies were, he
pulled himself up into a low crouch and
sprinted for the deeper growth of trees.

He was on top of the man in green before he
ever saw him, but the fellow paid no attention
to him, and stood looking intently away in the
direction of the approaching enemy. Bear
stumbled on a few steps farther and was
caught in the outspread arms of a strong figure,
who supported his stumbling body and gave
him a few reassuring claps on the back.

"It's all right, old man. You're safe now,"
came a quiet, deep voice.

"He looks done in," came another voice, in
deep, friendly tones.

"Get him over here and let him sit," came a
third.

Bear allowed himself to be led to a clearing,
where a cloak was spread out on the soft undergrowth, and he sprawled, gasping for

breath. He could still hear the faint pop of rifle
fire, although it seemed to be growing less, and
the green-clad figure he had run past a moment
before stepped smartly up to the tall man who
had caught him, and saluted.

"They won't risk coming farther, sir. They've
broken, and turned back."

"Good. I think they'll think twice before
coming into these woods again."

The man, who was apparently in charge of
the group that was scattered and spread out
among the trees and all but invisible in their
green cloaks, turned on his heel and strode up
to Bear.

"Now, old man, give us your tale. How came
you to be chased by those jackals? And how
have you crossed the lines unarmed?"

Bear looked up at the man, and studied his
face for the first time. It was a pleasant face,
weathered brown by the outdoors, and an open
smile played across the broad mouth. It was a
man's face, yet there was something about it
that reminded Bear of the elves when they sat
by the singing pools in Cypher and listened to
the songs and stories there.

Bear opened his mouth to speak, but a sudden dizziness evercame him, and the ground
spun beneath him, and he felt himself whirling
once more in a spinning dazzle of brilliant
lights, and a smooth blanket of darkness descended over him, deep and untroubled.

Vaguely, and from a great distance, he heard
the concerned voices for a moment, calling for
water, and a cloak, then the lights one by one

went out, and he felt himself floating gently on one of the small, fuzzy white clouds he had seen over the distant blue mountains. The voices faded, and he plunged into his old hammock in his dream, only now it seemed vague and far away. But the covers were deep and warm, and he was so very tired, and soon he knew nothing but the soft voice of sleep, singing its restful song over again until he was deep in a long, unbroken blue world, beyond harm, or hunger, or even dreams.

A TIMELESS JOURNEY

⊠ As Kore the Root moved away from the
companions on the bank of the Under Tide, he
thought it odd that the waters had been so disturbed. In all his lifetime there below the earth,
he had never visited the Under Tide when it
flowed with such fury. But he said nothing to
the odd strangers who were bent upon finding
their way outside into the chaos and havoc of
that unimaginable world aboveground.

Kore shuddered deep within himself, and
hurried along as best he could, to rejoin his
brothers far below the suffocating smell of open
air. He had not gone far when the deeper rumbling began, both behind and below him.

And somewhere above him, in a silent room,
Dwarf strained to hear what the ancient dwarfish walls were saying. It was silence, but then
not, and Broco couldn't decide if the noise

were nothing more than a tiny roaring in his
own ears.

In another moment, Ned and Cranfallow
were both alert, and sitting staring with
puzzled faces at Dwarf.

"I don't know what to make of it," he answered, reading the questioning looks. "I
thought it was just my ears, but it seems to
have grown louder now."

"You doesn't think this has nothing to do
with them dark things and that golden pool,
does you?" asked Cranny, his eyes wide and
staring.

"I don't know, old fellow," lied Dwarf, trying
not to disturb his friends with the visions of his
dream. "I'm not sure at all what it means, but
I'm certain it's time we all got started away
from here. Let's find what we can, and go on
now."

"I is with you, sir," said Ned, settling his hat
firmly onto his head and scrambling up.

Cranfallow had put his ear to the floor, as he
had seen Dwarf do on occasion, and listened
intently. "It almost sounds as if it was a river
run wild, like you hears sometimes up canyons,
where there's a snow melt running onto a
stream."

Broco bent low, and listened for a moment.
"It's water, Cranny, but I don't like the sound
of it. Something may have broken when the
Guardians were released. There was a lot of
noise and strain then. Some part of the Delving
may have been overloaded. It sounds as if the
water is spilling out of somewhere faster than it

should, at any rate. Much too fast." Dwarf hastily gathered up the rucksack he had packed with the travel cakes, and the sturdy, broad-bladed ax. "Let's gather our rations, and see if we can't find a way out of here."

"We is with you proper there," grumbled Ned, stuffing the contents of his pack down tightly and closing the drawstring.

"We is ready," said Cranfallow, drawing his own loaded pack onto his back and strapping two water skins across his shoulders.

Broco checked the fit of his comrades' rucksacks, and Ned in turn checked his, and heavily laden with their new supplies, the three friends marched briskly through the old armory, and beyond, where the pale blue light once more began to falter and vanish, and where a strange, troubled murmur seemed to go on in unending snoring notes.

Dwarf halted at the last fringe of light. "It's all something or other about roots, or the rest of the roots, still. I can't quite get the drift of it."

"Does this hole look like it are going up topsides?" asked Ned, settling the weight more evenly upon his back.

"It leads to the crossroad, if I recall my diagrams right. And the crossroad had something to do with the water. I think the underground stream is what actually takes you up."

"Well, it don't matter none. Just so longs as old Ned can pokes his snout out in good fresh air soon, it's all the better."

As the trio marched on, the light failed slowly, until they were once more in total

darkness. Broco now guided them by the feel of
the tunnel wall and the murmuring noise that
grew louder as they once more moved in the
blackness of the deep shafts. When the light
went, the sound grew much louder.

Dwarf took a firmer grip on the hefty ax, and
stumped on, his hat jammed down hard over
his ears, his other hand touching the small
bulge beneath his cloak where the Chest lay
next to his heart.

He had not gone far when the smooth floor
and walls began to tremble and shake, and a
fine layer of stone dust began filling the blank
darkness of the tunnel. The first tremor had
knocked the companions off their feet, and
Cranfallow cried out sharply as a portion of the
wall near him crashed to the floor only a few
paces in front of him. The utter darkness made
the noise more terrifying, and Ned grabbed for
Broco's hand as the sickening tremors went on,
rumbling and shivering, in stronger and stronger jolts.

"We is for it," cried Crannȳ, his voice flat
with horror now, although he was oddly
resigned in the face of this certain death.

"Here, Ned, Cranny, to me," shouted Dwarf,
and he struggled to hold his footing, and ex-
tended his hands to his friends.

Ned Thinvoice and Cranfallow threw their
outstretched arms around their small friend,
and clung to each other desperately as the
earth's trembling grew more violent.

"I knowed it weren't no good when them
things went down that well back there," com-

plained Ned wildly, "and I is sure we ain't got no longer than a squashed fly left to the poor blighters that we is."

"Hold, Ned," shouted Dwarf. "We still have the Chest."

"A fat lot of good that is agoing to do us here," answered Cranny. "What we needs is a lot of miles atween us and this here place, but I reckon we ain't agoing to gets no chance to does that now."

Dwarf struggled to free the tiny object from his cloak. As he removed the Arkenchest from its hiding place, a new and more dreadful sound reached the friends' ears, and even Dwarf, who held the hope-giving wonder of the Circle in his hands, felt his heart quail, and the dark certainty of their fate roared with the unchecked torrent of the tons of rushing water that exploded into their hearing, its din and thunder drowning all chance of speaking or saying their farewells to each other.

In a single, flashing split second, the friends gripped each other tightly, and then the crushing, suffocating flood of wild, raging water swept them into unknowing silence and a darkness that was deeper yet than mere absence of light.

Dwarf's last thought before the veil dropped was the utter despair at the knowledge that not only had he failed his friends and the Circle, but he had been the cause of the loss of the Arkenchest. Without the Secrets the Chest held, he knew Atlanton Earth would soon be darker than the onrushing black sea that at that moment devoured him.

But then at the very last, before the arms of darkness drew him into its being, he remembered the dream, and even as the light of one world failed, he saw the bright beginnings of the new and the outstretched arms of the white-robed figure of the strange Master beckoning to him lovingly.

And at the roaring, stormy edge of the Under Tide, Otter and Flewingam, and Thumb and his band, found themselves swept away into the wet blackness of that river, and time and life stood still on the brink of a heartbeat, as the friends were washed into the roaring tunnel of light that spiraled away into a great, towering sheet of white fire that touched the very hem of all Creation.

In their silent, unknowing flight, the companions grew once more together, and in that timeless journey, they found themselves once more in the same Breath of the All, and the Flame of Windameir burned brightly within them. It would be but a simple breath upon the heart, a brief thought, and they would awaken once more, to continue their long and perilous errand upon the changing faces of the Meadow Universes of Windameir.

The candle flame flickered suddenly in the wind, but the Light did not perish, nor vanish away forever, and even as the stillness grew, the Song of Life and Love was beginning its being anew.

The Starfishers Trilogy

__**SHADOWLINE**
by Glen Cook   (E30-578, $2.95,
The first book in The Starfishers Trilogy starts with the ven-
detta in space. They were the greatest fighting fleet in the
universe—battling betrayal and revenge, and the terrible
fate that awaited them on the edge of SHADOWLINE.

__**STARFISHERS**
by Glen Cook   (E30-155, $2.95,
The second volume in this trilogy, *Starfishers* is science
fiction the way you like it. They were creatures of fusion
energy, ancient, huge, intelligent, drifting in herds on the
edge of the galaxy, producing their ambergris, the sub-
stance, precious to man and the man-like Sangaree alike.

__**STAR'S END**
by Glen Cook   (E30-156, $2.95,
The final book: The fortress on the edge of the galaxy was
called Stars' End, a planet built for death—but by whom?
It lay on the outermost arm of the Milky Way, silent
cloaked in mystery, self-contained and controlled...unti
...a sinister enemy approaches from the depths of the galaxy, in hordes as large as a solar system. And its mission is
only to kill...

A MIND-BENDING FORAY INTO ADVENTURE AND DANGER!

___OUTLAND__

by Alan Dean Foster (E95-829, $2.75)
Even in space, the ultimate enemy is man. In orbit from Jupiter in view of its malignant red eye is OUTLAND. Here on Io—moon of Jupiter, hell is space—men mine ore to satisfy the needs of Earth. They are hard men, loners for whom the Company provides the necessities: beds, food, drink and women for hire. Now, in apparent suicide or in frenzied madness, the men are dying.

___2150 A.D.__

by Thea Alexander (E33-056, $2.95)
The brilliant, futuristic novel that explains a new way to live—macro-philosophy. It's a mind-expanding exodus from the imperfect today into a better tomorrow. Discover the beauty and the emotional demands such a journey can bring. This is a novel you can't put down, and a philosophy that can change your life.